The Old Man

Red Ridge Chronicles Book 7

Sarah Lamb

A thank you to my proofreader, Brooke, and all of the lovely women who help ARC read to catch those typos I miss!

This book was not written by AI. Any typos are proudly (and embarrassingly!) my own human created ones!

Paperback ISBN: 978-1-960418-67-8

Large print ISBN: 978-1-960418-68-5

Contents

To each of the special people who have helped me bring this series and many of my other books to life: Brooke, for her on point suggestions and proofreading; Nancy, for her fantastic covers; Spencer, for his incredible narration; and you, dear readers, for your endless support. It takes a village, and I'd be lost without mine.

Chapter 1

1870s, Red Ridge, Oregon

"Excuse me, sir?"

Gus turned and tipped his hat to the timid-looking young lady in front of him. "Howdy," he told her. "Were you talking to me?"

"I was," the girl, for she wasn't much more than that, said. "I'm trying to get to my uncle's farm. Do you know where Jake Smith lives?"

"Why, sure do," Gus told her, and then pointed. "You're going to go that a-way. Take a left at the old red barn that caught fire about ten years ago and got tore down three Aprils before last. After you head past that, keep going past the dried-up creek, turn by the berry patch that's hidden in the poison sumac, and keep on going until you get to a pile of rocks.

"Just past there a spell, you'll find it. Now, if'n you come to the well don't no one use no more, then you done gone too far. Turn back around by the sassafras tree that lightning struck in fifty-three, because if you go any further, you might fall into the abandoned cave."

He hitched his thumbs into his waistband and rocked back on his heels. "Easy as that. You can't miss the place. Big ole place used ter be small."

"Errr." The young lady nodded, and gave him a nervous smile. "Thank you. I think."

"Sure, sure," Gus said, and continued on his way as he took in the town.

A horse and wagon rode through the middle of the street, the harness jangling and the driver keeping an eye on someone's chickens that had escaped their confines and were pecking around.

Several women in a cluster stood, looking at a length of fabric one was holding, and the blacksmith's hammer rang loudly. The smell of his soot tickled at Gus's nose.

In the distance, the shrieks and laughter in the schoolyard faded as the brass bell signaling the return to lessons rang. There was a lot happening in town. Seemed like not a year went past without a few new families arriving.

Good thing that young woman had asked for some directions. She might not find her uncle's place otherwise. Red Ridge sure had changed since he first arrived, almost forty years before. It had grown from three town buildings and a handful of folks trying to make something out of nothing to a thriving community, one where a body was proud to call home.

The town continued to expand and change. The people did too. Well, all but him. Gus wasn't quite sure if that was a good thing or not, but life needed constants. Things that could be relied on, like the sun rising each morning, and he was one of them.

It felt good to be helping someone new to town. That was something he was talented at. Among other things. Helping, shooting, ranching; why, he'd done it all in his many years on this earth.

Well, except for one thing. Which was why he was standing in front of Mrs. Glinda Stover's general store. Today was the day. He was going to do it. He was going to march right inside and invite her for a slice of pie and a coffee at the diner.

Gus drew in a deep breath. Too big. It set him coughing a spell, and once he got his sputters under control, he straightened his hat, started to breathe in deep but stopped himself, and strode right toward the door.

Then walked past it again as his nerves got the better of him.

What was he thinking? Glinda Stover was perfect. Beautiful. Smart. A little bit sassy if you got on her wrong side. A woman who could and did do everything and did it well, while entirely on her own. What good was an old coot like him to someone like her?

His head lowered, and his shoulders slumped. Nothing, that's what. Despite all the tall tales he told, about half of 'em weren't true. And the other half? Well, he'd had a little help with the roles he'd played. While that didn't change the fact that he'd done plenty and knew plenty, it likely wasn't enough for a woman like her. He didn't know what she wanted—women were sure confusing—but he bet it wasn't him.

Gus wheeled around, planning to head back to the ranch he helped manage with Hannah and Eli. He'd forever put her name first when he talked about who he worked for, because he'd been with her since she was a young married woman. Had helped look after her, and her young'un, Meg, and the babe before it was born.

Why, it had been him who'd had the idea to send after a gunslinger to protect them, when Hannah's no-good brother-in-law tried to steal the land that belonged to her unborn son and force Hannah to marry him.

Gus stopped and grinned then. Had he known she'd fall in love with that gunslinger, and the feller with her, he might have done it sooner. They were just what the other needed.

Wasn't a finer man than Eli Jones, and he loved Hannah and those kids more than anything. Claimed those little ones for his own almost the moment he laid eyes on them.

His friends who'd been there to help, and now lived in Red Ridge, Billy Madison, who'd saved the pastor's daughter from a kidnapping, and Gavin Jefferson, who ended up rescuing a woman and her siblings, were right fine too. And good friends.

Friends who'd encouraged him in all he'd ever done. But would they encourage this? Gus couldn't help but want a little piece of what those young folks had. Romance. Love. A partner.

He paused in front of the general store and looked in through the window. There she was, looking so pretty, wearing that flowered apron that brought out the blue in her eyes, and her hair all pulled back, but for that single tendril that always curled against her cheek, like a princess out of a fairy tale.

Didn't matter she was a little older than him. Love didn't care about that. Didn't care about wrinkles or aching knees. And his was sure aching. It would rain tomorrow; he knew that for a fact. Not once had his knee been wrong.

Except that one time. He'd thought it would just be a little rain. Turned out to be a gully washer.

Gus wasn't sure if he should walk inside or keep going past when Glinda glanced up and met his eyes. With a gulp, he reached toward the door. Might as well go in. Could even say hello. If he lost his nerve asking her for a bite, he could always just order some of those peppermints he liked. She'd never know the real reason he came in.

That he was madly, deeply in love with her, and had been since he first laid eyes on her.

"You gonna keep waiting or are you going in today?" Madge from the diner asked as she walked past.

Gus had a retort on his tongue when he glanced over, but realized she wasn't alone and hadn't been talking to him. As Lisa, the diner's cook, answered her, her words flying away in the wind, he turned his attention back to the general store.

Even with it being the smaller of the two in town, it still kept busy. Matter of fact, it was the only general store Gus and his friends went to. Glinda had been the only one willing to sell to Hannah when Carson had been after her, and her willingness to help the other woman wouldn't ever be forgotten. Glinda had always had a special spot in Gus's heart, but that right there...it made him love her all the more.

Her voice was as gentle as a summer breeze. Her hair was the color of moonlight. He bet it would shimmer like it, too. Though she was a little shorter than him, she was as strong as that mule he owned back in '43. Too bad it had fallen into a gopher hole and lamed itself. That was one thing Glinda hadn't ever done, broken a leg. Both of hers were just as fine and sturdy as they could be, he thought, judging by the way she walked everywhere.

Yes, indeed, Glinda Stover was the most perfect of women. If only he weren't so dang scared to tell her so.

"Good morning, Gus," one of the women who worked at the hotel said as she passed by.

"Morning," he answered automatically, though his eyes didn't leave the large glass window of the store.

Just beyond, he could see Glinda walking around, straightening up this and that. He swallowed hard. He wanted to do it. Wanted to walk in, say hello. Buy something and make small talk. Ask her out.

But every time Gus tried to add on that last part, his tongue shriveled up and his voice croaked and he lost every bit of the nerve he had.

He sighed and tugged on his battered Stetson. Should he still try? Or just head back to the ranch? There was always something to check on or mend. It kept a man busy, mind and body.

"Can't wait forever," Pastor Blackstone said, as he walked past.

Gus scowled, his eyes narrowing, but then realized the man wasn't talking to him, as he continued to speak, reading from the paper before him, while making dramatic hand gestures.

"Our days are numbered. By delaying, we... No, that isn't the right word." The pastor's voice faded as he turned a corner, no doubt practicing for a sermon.

Another sigh pulled itself from Gus. Didn't matter what the pastor's words might be indicating. They were true enough to apply to his situation as well. He wasn't getting any younger. His mind might be sharp as a tack, but his body wasn't as spry. His joints ached and creaked, and things he used to do right easily were becoming difficult. Not that he'd tell anyone. But it sure did feel nice to have a full crew around the ranch again, doing the bulk of the work and letting him manage what needed looking after.

A customer left the general store, a basket on her arm, and he recognized Callie. Must have been getting some more of those books to write her stories in. Right fine writer, she was. He'd had the pleasure of listening to her read some of Hannah and Eli's story she'd written down.

But time was a'wasting. He couldn't stand there ruminating on everyone and everything. There was no excuse today to go into Glinda's store. His weekly newspapers weren't there. He didn't need more sweets. Hannah had all her supplies, and Eli didn't need nothing neither.

Gus straightened up, pushed off the side of the building he'd been against, and headed on shaky legs toward the store.

Didn't matter he was as nervous as the new horse at the livery. Today was the day. He was going to declare his affection for Glinda Stover. And if she broke his heart? Well, he'd survive. He had before.

Chapter 2

Her eyes had locked with Gus's, but he hadn't walked in. Glinda Stover tried to swallow down her disappointment as she'd seen him nod at her, then walk away. He hadn't gone far, and leaned against a building, as though he were watching her.

A hand went absently to her hair, pushing back the piece that always fell from her hairpin. Did she have an excuse to invite him over? Some new thing to show him? Something that needed fixing?

"Anything else?" Betty, her niece, asked.

"Another dozen of the teas that are so popular," Glinda said, returning her attention to the task at hand. She leaned overtop a wooden crate as she dug through it. "And be sure to order tins of those fancier sweets. We will be approaching Christmas soon, and those always sell well.

With the snows that come, I always order them early, so folks on the edge of town who don't come to town often can get them before the weather hits."

"We ought to get some other small items that make for good gifts," Betty said, looking up from the notepad she was writing the order on. "Hand mirrors, pretty hairpins, pocketknives? Perhaps extra flannel and yarn as well."

"That's a fine idea." Glinda straightened up, grimaced as she put a hand to her lower back, and said, "The schoolteacher always gives a peppermint stick to the children, and Pastor Blackstone does one for each person on Christmas Eve services, so go ahead and get an order in for three cases. And two of the penny candy as well."

"Yes, Aunt Glinda."

Glinda picked up a few spools of ribbon and headed toward the shelf where she kept them. As it usually did, pride filled her when she took the time to look around her store properly.

She'd sectioned it off into little areas. There was a large table with fabric, thread, trim, and notions. Near one of the windows was a large shelf with books to read, books to write in, and pencils and pens. She had an area each for hand tools, kitchen tools, cookware, gifts, fancy soaps, and gardening items. If a body wanted it, she had it or could get it from the catalog up under her counter.

Not bad, for starting ground up.

When Glinda had married as a young woman and moved here in a wagon train with her new husband, Richard, she'd never imagined owning a store. The two of them had set out to buy land, raise livestock, and make a living as homesteaders. Richard had a way with woodworking, so he'd started to build this place as their home, while he hunted for acreage.

Theirs hadn't been a love match. Richard had come into the restaurant she cooked at a few times, always treated her well, and one day told her he was leaving the following day for Oregon. If she wanted to marry him and cook for him he'd be sure to take care of her the rest of his days.

If only she'd known how few they'd be.

Still, for a young woman with no chance for anything more? It was an offer she was happy to take. The opportunity to have something to change her future, and with a man who was kind, was far more than she'd ever hoped for. Glinda had said yes and never looked back.

She wondered, sometimes, if they'd had a chance to grow old together, would there have been love? She'd never experienced it herself, but it had made her niece happy. Funny how someone could get a hankering for something they'd never had before.

It wasn't long after they'd arrived in Red Ridge, however, that he took sick with pneumonia and died, leaving Glinda, and the babe in her, alone. Glinda had very little money, and that meant she wouldn't be able to fully repay the loan he'd taken for the lumber and the in-town plot of land. Richard had intended to sell the place to someone else once they'd moved to their homestead, but with him now gone, Glinda knew it could serve a better purpose.

A store.

With little more than ingenuity, grit, and her few dollars, Glinda found people to help her finish the building, and then she stocked the shelves, worked her fingers to the bone, and went from a young, frightened widow to a proud shop owner. A half-dozen years later, the Olstens moved to Red Ridge and opened a much larger general store, but Glinda hadn't fretted. Instead, she continued to provide exceptional service to her customers, the majority of whom stayed with her.

Payment by payment, Glinda repaid the loan Richard had taken out, raised her boy, and when he grew and married, moving a few hours' ride away, she'd been able to still provide for herself and put a little by for a rainy day. Of course, having Betty here was a blessing, and it had worked out well for her niece as well.

"Gus is still outside," Betty said, as she passed the front window. "I do wish he'd come in and not stare. It makes me feel so bad for him."

Glinda sighed, though she also smoothed her hands down her apron. "It's a wonder he manages to speak to me half the time."

"I was sure grateful he watched over us when the store was broken into," Betty said. "I feel like him having a reason to be here made him feel more comfortable. Less shy."

"Yes," Glinda agreed. "And I was very glad to have him here. What a difficult time that was."

What Glinda would never admit was that for a time she'd wondered if she'd be able to keep the store open, what with the worry over staying safe and protecting Betty. Thankfully, the sheriff, his friends, the hotel owner, and Gus had looked after them. The men causing the trouble had been removed, and things had been quiet ever since.

Still, she had trouble shaking the feeling that was about to change.

"I wonder if you two will ever be more than friends," Betty said, crossing the store to check how many bars of soap were for sale.

That was something she wondered as well. Glinda wasn't exactly sure where she and Gus stood. They were friends, and sometimes she got the feeling he thought of them as more, but it was rare that they spent much time together outside of her store. There had been a few meals at the hotel with Betty and Kent, then once or twice at the diner with them, but that was really it.

If things didn't progress soon, they never would, she figured. She worried she was at the point in life where there was more behind her than in front. That had never really bothered her before. She'd spent so much time raising her son and running her store, there wasn't much left at the end of the day to do or be anything but exhausted.

However, when her son had moved away, marrying a young woman he'd been corresponding with, and then Betty had come along to help her, Glinda couldn't help but wish she had just a little bit of special company in the evenings, like the young folks did.

"Foolish sentiment, that's all," she muttered to herself.

The door swung open just then, and in walked Hannah.

"Where are those children of yours?" Glinda asked with a smile. "It's been too long since I last saw them."

"Mrs. Blackstone is minding them for me while I come in here," Hannah said, tiredly handing over a list. "Benjamin is getting into everything nowadays, and the baby still isn't sleeping much at night."

"Those days will pass by quickly," Glinda said, remembering them all too well. "But I don't have to tell you that."

Hannah gave her a warm smile. "No, and I enjoy each moment. Even if it is a bit exhausting some days." She glanced around and said, "I thought I saw Gus outside as I was walking this way. Did he not come in? I have the wagon and could take him back. I didn't realize I needed anything or I'd have asked him to come in my place. I know he loves to keep busy in town so he can say his own hellos."

"No, he's not come in today," Glinda said briskly, as she busied about, setting Hannah's requested items out.

"I might be overstepping," Hannah said, "especially as I don't really know how you feel, but I know he likes you a good deal."

"Sure has a funny way of showing it," Betty said. "Hello, Hannah."

Hannah laughed. "Yes, he does. Hello, Betty. But I do know he was a little sad when that old friend of your family's had come through a while back, and you had dinner at the hotel with him. He moped for days until he realized it wasn't a beau."

"Here you are, dear," Glinda said, loading Hannah's basket. She accepted the money, gave a few coins in change, and said, "Who can say how a man thinks?"

The younger women laughed at the comment, as she'd hoped they would, but Glinda couldn't help but search through the window for Gus. Her stomach sank in disappointment when she didn't see him anywhere. Perhaps he'd gone home.

It took a good deal of effort not to sigh. Even if he only stopped in for a moment, it always brightened her day. But, it wasn't to be. No visit today, no flutters she tried to tamp down.

Maybe for her, there wouldn't be any romance or even a glimpse of it ever. She might be an older woman, but that didn't mean she didn't still want someone to spend time with and enjoy. However, she also knew if it wasn't with Gus, she didn't want it at all.

Chapter 3

"...and the calf was half in, half out the fence, its backside stuck, while its mother was shouting at the top of her lungs." Eli shook his head. "Like to know how they keep breaking that one part of the fence. Only right there. I think we've fixed it a half-dozen times in as many weeks."

"Reckon you oughter not get your fence boards that place you been getting them. Seem weak," Gus said, reaching for the gravy.

"Billy said the same," Eli answered, as he dropped two biscuits on his plate. They made a clanking sound, and Gus could see the char on the bottoms. "Also promised to come and take a look and see what I'm doing wrong with the fence."

"You got me if he can't help." Gus poured the white gravy overtop his biscuits, and then on the porkchop and mashed potatoes Hannah had made until his plate was near swimming in it.

"Here you go," Meg said at his elbow, passing him the green beans.

"Thank you, missy," Gus told her, heaping a mess of them on his plate. "And for these fine biscuits you made, too."

Meg watched, beaming, as he took a bite, and let out a loud grunt of satisfaction. "You like 'em? Even with the black on the bottom?"

"Might just be the tastiest I've ever had. No offense to your mama," he added.

Meg let out a giggle, and little Ben, who was on Hannah's knee, laughed too, though he was too young to be talking. "I'm glad you are eating with us tonight," she said, picking up her fork.

"Same," Hannah said. "You are welcome every day, but I know you like to be in the bunkhouse sometimes."

"Got to keep an eye and an ear on things," Gus told her. "That's my job."

It was true. He might feel part of Hannah's family, and he'd sure claim them, but hired hands, even those working for a former gunslinger, could get lazy if they weren't looked after proper. And that was something Gus couldn't allow. Not after the trouble Hannah had been through.

By being with the other men, he also got a good sense of who they were. Eli was also a good judge of character, and so far there'd been no issues with the men, but Gus didn't plan to take any chances.

Talk at the table turned from fences to the upcoming marriage of Callie and Ryan.

"Are you ever gonna get married?" Meg asked Gus suddenly, her eyes wide. "Seems everyone's getting it. Like spring fever, Mrs. Blackstone says. Or something in the water."

Hannah quickly scolded, "Meg, that's not polite to talk about."

"I don't mind," Gus answered mildly. "No, don't reckon I will, least not any time soon," he told Meg. "I like being around here. Wouldn't want to leave."

"She could come here," Meg said, her mouth full. "Maybe help Ma, like you help Pa."

Gus could see Hannah and Eli glance at each other.

"Meg, can you go check on the baby?" Eli asked.

Gus tilted his head and didn't hear anything, but Meg's face lit up, and she ran out of the room, eager to do as told. She loved caring for the new one and was a right little mother to it.

"Sorry," Eli said. "She doesn't mean anything by it."

"I know," Gus said. "Couldn't never be upset at her."

"Meg just wants you to be happy. We all want that," Hannah said.

Gus nodded but didn't answer. He looked down at his plate, feeling that familiar squeeze in his stomach that started up each time he thought about wanting to tell Glinda just how much he cared for her.

"You've got our support if you do want to be with someone," Hannah said softly. "Even if you need to leave here."

"Not telling no one nothing," Gus said gruffly. "Especially when there's nothing to tell."

"Of course not," Eli said quickly. "A man's got to have his personal business personal."

"But what if—" Hannah broke off, as the sound of the baby crying filled the kitchen. She handed Benjamin to Eli, who started to bounce him on his knee.

"Sorry," Eli muttered. "Hannah..." He shook his head.

"Just wants to make sure everyone's looked after," Gus answered for him. "Makes this old man feel proud to have someone who cares. Lot of folks don't have that. I've got a whole bunch of you."

"Sure do," Eli said. "And you don't have to worry about my prying. But if you ever need anything or want someone to ask opinions of, I'm always nearby."

"Appreciate it," Gus said, and tucked into his pork chop. They ate in silence for a moment, then he ventured, "You reckon I'm too old to be thinking about a woman? If there was one, I mean."

Eli studied him for a moment, then shook his head. "Nope. What I reckon is that any woman in this town would be lucky to have you. A woman wants a man who is steady, mature, reliable. And if it's the one I think you might have your eye on, well, I know for a fact she likes you and is looking for just that."

Gus sat up just a little straighter. "Well, there's a lot to like," he said. Then he quickly added, "If a man was looking to find a little romance, I mean. Not saying I am. I'm happy here."

"And we're happy with you," Hannah said, walking in and leaning over to kiss his cheek. "But I won't be selfish and keep you all to myself, if the time comes."

"I will," Meg said, clambering up into her chair. "You let me win at checkers."

Everyone laughed. Gus gave her a wink and tugged on the braid hanging over her shoulder.

Settling herself with the baby in her arms, Hannah asked, "Could one of you men do me a favor tomorrow? It's my washing day, so I'd rather not leave home, but I forgot to get a sack of cornmeal. I thought I had plenty, but I don't."

"Billy and I are going to get that fence fixed in the morning," Eli said. "Would you be willing, Gus?"

"Sure, I'll take the wagon over. Need anything else?" Gus asked.

Hannah grew a thoughtful look on her face. "Might have you get me two sacks. If we get a little extra each week to set by for winter, it will be a help to us later, and also not strain Mrs. Stover's supplies. You might tell her that's my plan. Though, it means you'll have to go a little more often for me."

Gus nodded as a little whisper of excitement tickled at him. Now he had an excuse to go to Glinda's store. He just hoped if she asked him why he hadn't stopped in, after they'd glanced at each other through her window, he'd have thought up a good excuse. Maybe he could say something about the fence. That he was distracted.

Or, maybe she'd not ask, and he wouldn't have to worry about it. She was a right polite woman. Never made a body feel bad about nothing. Gus finished his dinner, tucked into the apple cobbler set in front of him, and then played a close match of checkers with Meg besting him before heading back to the bunkhouse.

Inside, the men were teasing one of the newer hands, Clark, a man of thirty, who'd been writing a mail-order bride and got her photo today.

"Everyone's got something to offer," Clark grunted, raising his chin, and snatching back the woman's photograph from one of the younger hands who'd been looking at it. "Just because you don't see it, doesn't mean it's not there. She's not so bad. Anyway, not like you have anyone writing you letters."

"Let me see," Gus said.

Clark almost reluctantly handed over the picture, while some of the other men snorted. Gus studied her carefully. The woman wasn't too much to look at, but Gus nodded as he gave back the photo. “That there’s a woman with some kind eyes. I bet she smiles a lot.”

“Cooks good, she said,” Clark told him, reading from the letter. “Likes to read.”

“So do you,” Gus said. He patted the man’s shoulder. “And you like to eat. It’s a good place to start. Now, you others got something to do other than hassle him over his personal affairs?”

The ranch hands quickly made excuses and scattered, a few going to their bunks, while others sat with quiet occupations. After giving Gus a grateful look, Clark sat at a table with a pencil and paper and busied himself writing his new sweetheart.

Gus settled himself with a mug of coffee and his thoughts. Glinda had kind eyes. She smiled a lot too. A woman like that, with the difficulties like she’d had could have let life harden her. Not her. She was like his favorite pocketknife. Sharp, steady, and had always been there.

But what if she got tired of that? What if she wanted more? Gus frowned. She wouldn’t ever consider one of those mail-order matches, would she? Maybe he’d best make it known he was interested in her.

If only it weren’t so hard. Back when her store had been broken into, he’d almost confessed. Asked her to marry him then and there to protect her. He wouldn’t let anyone hurt her, he’d said, and he’d meant that, as he sat in front of her store, rifle in his lap, and eyes in all directions. Weren't no one getting through him.

Why hadn't he said something when he had the chance? Gus shook his head and drained his mug. Tomorrow. He'd try again tomorrow.

Chapter 4

After stowing the broom in the little niche along the wall, Glinda flipped the store sign to open, and then greeted the stranger who walked in first. "Good morning."

He nodded but didn't answer and started a slow circle of the store. She tried not to think of his behavior as too odd. They got a few individuals like that, with as much traffic as the hotel got. Usually, however, they did return her welcome.

"Can I help you find anything?" she asked, looking directly at him.

"Not right now, thanks," the man told her, opening the lid of a barrel to look inside.

Glinda nodded, though a strange prickle was on her arms. She glanced down to see goosebumps. That was odd. It wasn't the least bit cold in her store. She'd lit the fire to chase away the morning chill and heat her kettle almost an hour ago. Was there something about the man her body was trying to signal to her about? As a woman alone, she'd learned to be aware of such sensations.

She returned behind the counter, straightening here and there and pulling out a rag to dust, but everything was already tidy and clean. No matter. She just wanted the distraction so she could observe the stranger.

Betty wasn't there this morning. She and Kent had taken the trip about two hours away to another town to get some items that had been delivered there to their hotel instead of to his. Glinda had felt more than comfortable managing whatever customers came into her store. But now she was having doubts. This man was making her nervous, even though he wasn't doing anything but looking around.

The door opened again, and a few customers came in. One to sell her eggs and butter, another for an order she was picking up. Lisa from the diner dropped off their list, while the barber came in for some more shaving soap.

Relieved not to be alone, Glinda helped each, though her eyes found their way to the stranger frequently. He was perhaps forty, not too tall, still with a good bit of hair on his head. He was dressed well, with boots that were shiny, a pair of clean dark trousers, and a checked button-down shirt that bore no evidence of stains.

When the last customer left, Glinda opened her mouth to ask the man how she could help him when he approached.

Without any preamble, he said, "Are you Glinda Stover?"

"I am," she told him. "I own this store. You have me at a disadvantage, sir. Who are you?"

"Charles Wimer." He glanced around once more, then shook his head. "Begging your pardon, ma'am, you just aren't the sort of person I'd have taken for being dishonest. I'm not quite sure the best way to handle this."

"Dishonest?" Glinda snapped her jaw shut and stood to her full height, even though it was a few inches shorter than the man before her. "I beg *your* pardon. I am many things, Mr. Wimer, but I am not dishonest. Has there been some sort of complaint made against me?"

The door opened again, and Winnie, the sheriff's wife, walked in. The man said, "I'll be outside looking around. We will discuss this once your customer is gone."

He strode away, and Glinda found herself sputtering a hello to Winnie.

"Is everything all right?" Winnie asked. "You seem a little flustered. Did that man do something?"

"Yes, he...he just accused me of being dishonest!" Glinda said, not sure if they were tears of anger or of hurt that were trying to spring free. "In all my days, never has anyone said such a thing about me!"

"He obviously doesn't know what he's talking about," Winnie told her, reaching out a hand to squeeze hers. As she released it, she added, "I'm sure it's all a misunderstanding."

"I imagine you are right," Glinda said, forcing herself to take a few slow breaths. It helped a little. She glanced toward the window, where she could see Mr. Wimer walking around the side of her store. "I'm going to speak with him once I've helped you."

"Then let me just drop my list off," Winnie said, setting it on the counter. "Nothing is urgent. I'll come by later. Do you want me to go get Gavin?"

Glinda thought about it for a moment, then shook her head. "No, dear, but thank you. Hopefully, he goes as quickly as he came."

"All right. Good luck," Winnie added as she walked toward the door.

After a quick look at it, Glinda weighted the list down so it wouldn't blow away and be forgotten, and then stepped outside after Winnie just a moment later. From the corner of her eye, she saw the woman walking over to the church gardens. As she glanced around, Glinda spotted Mr. Wimer headed around the back of her store, jotting something down on a notepad.

"Excuse me," she said firmly, marching up to him, her skirts bustling about her and her apron strings flapping. "What do you think you are doing?"

He didn't bother to look up as he answered. "I'm seeing if the plans I drew might actually work."

"Plans? What plans?" She tried to see what he was writing, but couldn't make it out.

"For my resort," the man answered. "Once I knock down this building, and buy the space behind it, I'll be putting in a resort and a spa. A lot of folks would pay good money for that sort of thing around here."

Glinda found herself sputtering again, in a most unladylike, and most unlike her way, before she managed to gasp, "Knock down my store? I don't think so! Just what gives you the right? Nothing! Nothing at all!"

Mr. Wimer looked at her then, and crossed his arms over his chest. "I own this land, Mrs. Stover. So, I have every right."

"You do not!" Glinda said, her voice rising in volume. "Every penny of this place I paid off! Why, the last payment was made years ago."

"No, it wasn't," Mr. Wimer said, just as firmly. "My family took over your loan payments when they stopped. My lawyer is arriving in town soon. We'll be staying at the hotel. He has the proof with him, since I figured you wouldn't believe it from me. Once he gets here and things are settled before the law, we start construction."

"We will see about that!" Glinda said. "You won't be getting away with this. Such lies!"

"Do whatever you want," Mr. Wimer said with a shrug. "It won't change things. This is my land, has been that way for a few years, and you are trespassing and here illegally. The building, the goods, all of it. It's mine."

"This is the first I'm hearing of such a thing," Glinda told him. "There's been some mistake, I'm sure. I—"

"Will be talking with my lawyer," the man told her. "I'm not here to argue with you. I have the proof, and nothing that you can say or do will stop me from knocking this place down and building my hotel. But I'm doing this all legal-like, which is why I'm waiting for my lawyer."

He gestured then to the front of her store where she could see Gus and Gavin at the door. "Looks like you have a few customers. Best take care of them while you still can. In a week, you'll be out of there, and there's nothing you can do to stop it. Dishonesty has its price, ma'am, and you'll be paying it."

Chapter 5

The sound of Gavin's violin was right soothing. Gus leaned back, his eyes half closed and his feet propped on a stool there in the sheriff's office. The man had a way of saying all the things a fellow thought, but with his fingers and some strings.

As the song came to a close, the words tumbled from Gus's mouth before he could catch them. "Danced with a woman once to that song. Was the day before she broke my heart."

"I'm sorry. Had I known, I wouldn't have played it," Gavin said, setting his instrument on top of his desk.

"Was a long time ago," Gus grunted. "Hardly remember her nowadays."

"That so?" Gavin fixed him with a look. Gus knew it well. Those gunslingers all had it. Meant they wanted to hear more, and you'd best not stop talking. It wasn't something he minded at all. His life was full of stories; he was always happy to share. Even the difficult ones. Could be they'd help someone else, somehow.

"Back in thirty-seven, it were," Gus said. "We was engaged." He let out a barky laugh. "You young pups might not have recognized me back then. Stood tall and straight. Had bigger muscles, and moved a little quicker."

"We all slow down as we get older," Gavin answered mildly. "What happened?"

Gus let his eyes wander. First to the jail calls, then to the window, and then to the past. "I don't rightly know. When I asked her to marry me, she was real excited. But the day came, and I waited at the church. Waited all day. She never came. I went home, feeling about as low as a man can. Come to find out, she'd run off with a cowboy, for the same outfit I'd been working on."

If he thought hard enough, he could remember her face. Heart-shaped, with hair the color of the dust that settled on his trousers. The smell of her. Lye soap and rosewater to cover it. The way that he'd pledged his heart, but she hadn't done the same. Gus shook his head, loosening the memories so they flew away.

"Love can be painful," Gavin said. His own eyes were unfocused. "And confusing. Very confusing. Even married now, you'd think it would be easier. Some days, it's not."

"Slinging a gun or roping cattle is a lot simpler," Gus agreed sagely.

Gavin nodded. "I—" He sat up suddenly, a frown quickly forming.

The movement made Gus do the same, and he followed where the sheriff was looking, across the street. "What's going on?" Gus asked, squinting as he tried to see what had caught Gavin's attention. His eyes weren't as good as the younger man's.

"A guy came out of Mrs. Stover's store, and was walking around the side, writing stuff down. Never seen him before." Gavin drew himself to his feet and said, "I'm going over."

"I got to get some cornmeal for Hannah, so I'll join you," Gus said, already to the door. "Betty's not around, and if Glinda's got trouble, don't want her alone. Got nothing else to do, so I can stay a spell."

As they walked over, Gavin put a hand on his arm and said, "Before we get there, I want to tell you something."

"What's that?" Gus asked.

"That woman, she just wasn't right for you at all. She knew it, and was too scared to tell you. Didn't mean more than that, so don't let your past keep you from what you could have."

Gus didn't answer. Could that be the case? She was scared? Didn't know what else to do? He thought back to those days. He'd been hotter under the collar, quick to start something. Slow to let it go. Maybe...maybe Gavin was right.

Or, maybe he wasn't. At the time, Gus was a ranch hand, not a cowboy. Women had always liked cowboys. They came and went, were mysterious. Might be that he just wasn't good enough. Could even be Glinda thought the same, no matter what Eli had said the night before about women liking mature, steady men.

A sigh hovered, half in him half out, but then Gus focused on Glinda, who was coming out of the store and looking mighty upset. They were too far away to hear what was going on, but he and Gavin stepped a little quicker when her hands started waving, and loud, though indecipherable, words drifted toward them on the breeze.

"Don't like this," Gavin rumbled.

"Making the hairs on my arm stand up," Gus agreed. "You reckon something's going on?"

"Reckon I do."

Glinda caught sight of them then, and though Gus saw she was trying to smooth her expression, he saw the anger and fear and confusion all there at once, warring across her face. He didn't know what was going on, but wanted to save her from it.

"Glinda, what's happened?" he asked, reaching for her as she neared them and putting his arms on her elbows before he'd even realized it.

"Oh, it's terrible!" she said, on a half sob. "Gus, that man says he owns my land! And my store! And that I never paid off my loan." She sniffled, and her head dropped while one hand wiped at her cheeks.

She moved slightly closer to him, and Gus had never wanted to put his arms around anyone more than he wanted to do right now. Gus moved his hands up, so that one was around her shoulder, and he stood slightly to the side, his arm partially wrapped around her. "Start from the beginning," he told her. "We're gonna help."

She nodded, sniffling, and walked toward the store. "Inside, though. I won't give that man any more satisfaction of watching me get upset."

Gus held the door and followed her inside. Gavin shut and locked the door behind him, putting up the closed sign. Just beyond, Gus could see the stranger walking toward the hotel. He took a moment to study him. Gus might not know what was going on, but he was sure of one thing. Nobody would upset his Glinda. Not while he was still breathing.

That man, whoever he was, sure had a lot to answer for.

Chapter 6

Gus watched as Glinda fussed around making coffee. They'd told her she didn't have to, but Glinda had just shaken her head, then pressed a mug of coffee into his hands and the sheriff's. Once she'd returned the kettle to the stove in her store, Glinda took a deep breath. "I hardly know where to start."

For a woman who hardly anything ever shook, she was looking mighty rattled, and that was concerning Gus far more than he'd ever let on.

"Just say the first thing that comes to mind," Gus said. He added, hoping it sounded reassuring, "We're going to fix whatever's happening, I'm sure of that."

"I hope you can," Glinda said, "however, that man seems very sure of himself." She drew a deep breath as she smoothed her work apron and then pressed her hands to her stomach. “He claims that I stopped making payments on my loan and his family picked it up and paid it off several years ago. Therefore, my store and the land it’s on belong to him.”

“If that’s the case, why wait until now to tell you?” Gavin asked, cocking his head a little to the side.

“He plans to tear my store down—tear it down!—and build a resort and a spa. Whatever that is.”

“Don’t rightly know,” Gus grunted and rubbed at his ear. “Must be some fancy thing from back East.”

“They’ve them in the West too,” Gavin said grimly. “But that’s not something we want here in town. We don’t need that kind of thing inviting all those lookers-on, and all the trouble they might bring in. The type of folks who frequent those places are the well to do, who often look down on or cause difficulties for the locals.

“The resort is a fancy hotel with all kinds of special things for amusement. Concerts, stores, even gambling. The spa is for relaxation or health, including some beauty treatments, bathhouses, and things like that.”

“Bathhouses? You mean a whole house for a bath? I like to be as clean as the next man,” Gus grunted, crossing his arms in front of himself, “but that sounds excessive.”

“That many people? And gambling in our town? We don’t want that at all,” Glinda gasped. “Red Ridge needs to grow the proper way—with folks who want to live here and make something for themselves. Not be filled with those passing through. Why, that just invites criminals in!"

"Don't have to tell me that," Gavin said. "That's why I'm against it."

"Makes me wonder, though," Gus said, rubbing at his chin. "Surely your land ain't big enough for what he's wanting. He going after anyone else?"

"Good question," Gavin said. "I hadn't thought of that."

"As far as I am aware," Glinda said, "he's got his sights set on the plot behind mine. I'm not sure who owns it. For all I know, he's already bought it and pretending like he hasn't."

"Regardless," Gus said. "We need to send that fella packing."

"We need to get to the bottom of this first," Gavin said. "I doubt he'd make an accusation such as he did without proof to back it up. We need to see that before we accuse him."

"Now see here!" Gus started hotly.

But Glinda interrupted. "The sheriff is right. And I understand that might be the case. But such things can be forged, can't they?" At the sheriff's nod, she hesitantly added, "He said his lawyer had evidence and was coming to town. They are both staying in the hotel."

"I'd like to see what he has," Gavin said. "Ask my own questions."

"I'd appreciate it," Glinda said.

Gus grunted. "This here man got a name?"

"Charles Wimer," Glinda said. "He didn't say from where."

Gavin drained the last of his mug and stood from the too-small wooden chair Glinda had offered him. "Then I aim to find out. I'm heading to the hotel."

"I must find out what I can about my loan," Glinda said. "The bank promised to keep the deed secure for me. That's where I'm going. Only..."

"Only what?" Gus asked, when she didn't answer. He glanced at the shop door Gavin had just slipped through.

"I'm nervous," Glinda confessed. "What if they don't have it? I know I paid my loan off, but..." She shook her head, and a tear rolled down her cheek. "That man has me second-guessing myself."

"Now don't you worry none," Gus said. He stood as well. "I'll go over there with you, and we'll get this straightened out. That man's a stranger. You ain't. Sure as sure, the bank manager would be on our side."

"Oh, would you?" Glinda asked. "That is, I mean, I can't ask you to do that. You surely must have other things to do."

Gus shook his head. He wasn't about to mention the cornmeal Hannah wanted. Especially since he'd stumbled on a half-dozen sacks in the root cellar that morning. He knew it had likely just been to give him a reason to head into town. He'd get it when he needed an excuse to stop back in and knew Hannah would never say a word.

"Nope. Nothing's more important to me than helping you, making sure you're okay."

Two spots of red came into Glinda's cheeks just then, and Gus drew in a deep breath. He knew now wasn't the right time, but...

"You're important to me," he went on. "And I—"

The words dried up then, though Glinda's eyes were fixed on him, waiting. Gus reached for his mug, gulped down the last drops, and said, "I think we'd best go. Don't rightly know the bank hours."

Something akin to disappointment flashed across her face. Gus suspected it anyway, because that's sure what he was feeling right now. Why couldn't he say what he really wanted to?

As they went to the door, Gus paused. "There is something I want to say to you. I reckon we better get this straightened out first."

"Something, maybe over a meal at the diner?" Glinda asked.

Gus's chest puffed out a little. How'd she know? "Yes. And I'm hoping you'll join me there soon? Just the two of us?"

"I'd be delighted," Glinda said with a smile. "Thank you, Gus."

They stepped outside and walked together over to the bank. Though the situation was a dire one, Gus couldn't help but feel a little bit proud she was walking so close. He almost offered his arm, but worried it might be too soon.

Maybe when they were walking to or from the diner?

The bank wasn't far away, and Gus held open the door. The smell of paper and ink, wood polish and money tickled at his nose.

"Welcome, Mrs. Stover, Mr. Malone," the bank manager said, looking up from a desk behind some iron bars. How can I help you this fine day?"

"It isn't fine," Gus said. "Got us a problem, Mr. Logan."

"An enormous one," Glinda said. Her voice had a little wobble as the bank manager approached them. "You see, a Mr. Wimer has come, claiming that I didn't pay my loan and that my land and my store are his. You weren't the bank manager when it was done, some many years ago, but Mr. Thomas, the former bank manager, had it all written down in a ledger and also promised to keep my deed here, safe at the bank should I ever need it."

"Then all should be in order," Mr. Logan agreed, and walked to the wall where a row of ledgers sat. "Can you give me a general idea of when your final payment was made?"

"May of sixty-four," Glinda said confidently. "I remember perfectly because it was the same month and day as my boy's birthday."

The bank manager nodded, and went to the wall. He took down a book and ran his finger slowly through the columns. He shook his head and said, "I don't see it listed there. Let me go further back."

"Take your time," Glinda said, "but it's all there. I made those payments."

"I'm sure you did," Mr. Logan said.

He continued to look through the books on the wall, then moved to a door. "One moment. I'm just going to check for the deed. That might be simpler."

As soon as he vanished from sight, Gus snuck a look at Glinda. She looked terrified. "It's happening," she whispered. "Just as I feared. He can't find it."

"Now, we don't know that yet," he tried to reassure her, though he was secretly agreeing. This wasn't looking in Glinda's favor. Sometimes it didn't matter if a body was telling the truth, if there was no proof of it.

Mr. Logan returned, his hands empty. "Mrs. Stover, I'm sorry. I don't know what to tell you. It was about eight years prior to my coming here you claim that store and the land was paid off. However, I can't find a record of it."

"Claim? I'm not claiming anything!" Glinda said heatedly. "I made those payments. Mr. Thomas recorded them in front of my eyes."

"I believe you," Mr. Logan said, holding up a hand. "But I can't find it in my records. What he wrote it in, I don't have."

"Does that mean the land isn't mine? Where did all those payments go that I made?" Glinda was close to tears, and Gus placed a hand on her arm to try to comfort her.

Mr. Logan looked uncomfortable and tugged at his collar. "I see you made payments, Mrs. Stover. I see that in the ledgers from before sixty-three. However, in sixty-three and sixty-four, I see none. I don't know if they stopped, or why we don't have your deed. One can only assume that means we don't have a complete picture. Perhaps those books and the deed were damaged. Things do happen."

"They shouldn't, when you give your things to a bank to safeguard," Gus said, half in a growl. "So, you telling us she don't own what she done worked and sacrificed to pay for?"

"I'm saying," Mr. Logan answered, mopping at his brow with a handkerchief, "that I don't know.

"I am not a liar!" Glinda said, looking between him and the banker.

"No one is calling you one, but we're going to have to get to the bottom of this." Mr. Logan held up a hand. "Let me make inquiries. I'll find out where the old banker moved to. Perhaps he can help. There's nothing more I can do for you, I'm sorry."

Wordlessly, Glinda nodded and turned, walking to the door and looking such a terrible shade of pale Gus was worried she might fall over. As soon as they got outside, he said, "Don't you worry none."

"How can I not?" she asked, gesturing around her. "Red Ridge has been my home most of my life. I built that store from nothing. And now..."

"And nothing's going to happen to it," Gus told her. "You trust me, Glinda. I ain't gonna let nothing or no one run you out of there. You hear?"

Their eyes locked, and Gus couldn't help but be a little pleased at the pink that came to her cheeks again.

"Trust me," Gus said quietly, then hesitated and reached for her hand, cupping it. Though she worked hard, and it was a little rough in spots, he thought it the most wonderful thing to ever touch his skin.

"I do," Glinda whispered, so softly he could hardly hear it, since his good ear weren't too good no more. "I...I suppose I'd best return to the store."

"You do that," he said, reluctantly letting go of her. "I'll update the sheriff. But I'm stopping by to take you for lunch tomorrow. Betty'll mind the store."

"You don't have to do that," Glinda said, her cheeks now the color of Hannah's tomatoes she was growing. "I was just teasing."

"Well, I weren't," Gus said, straightening up a little bit. "The full course, Glinda. Coffee, lunch, and pie. All on me. Now, if you'd excuse me, I got some thinking to do."

He walked away then, managing to get himself out of sight before he leaned against a thick tree, gasping for air, one hand pressed to his chest. He'd done it. Sort of. Asked her. He just hoped he wasn't in the middle of dying from the fear that was consuming him.

He couldn't let Glinda's land and store be taken. He also couldn't let himself collapse from the fear of being alone with her.

"Always thought in my old age, I'd know how to do it all," Gus muttered to a rabbit that was hopping past. "Reckon even an old dog's got some new tricks he can learn."

Chapter 7

"I wish I'd never left," Betty said, pausing from where she was scooping coffee beans from a sack to fill a large glass jar. "I'm so sorry, Aunt Glinda. You shouldn't have been here alone. I feel terrible."

"Nonsense," Glinda said, though she'd wished for the same thing yesterday. "I've been just fine running this store since before you were born. You need to live your life. Spending time with Kent is part of that. Besides, you were on a very important errand. The order needed to be picked up, and your young man was quite glad of your company and the chance to be alone with you for a while."

"I know, but I still feel badly," Betty sighed. She placed the jar lid on gently.

"*I'll* feel badly if he does manage to get this place," Glinda said. "My boy doesn't want anything to do with it, and I know how much you love it. It's been my every intention to give it to you one day. I've a bit set by for his inheritance."

"Don't you worry about that right now," Betty said. "You aren't going anywhere, and neither is this store." She reached into a crate and pulled out several small boxes, displaying them in the glass-front case. Inside each of the boxes was a lovely brooch, something both of them were sure would sell quickly for Christmas.

But would she even be here then? What about when the first snow fell? It felt as though time were moving far faster than she'd ever imagined it could.

"I do, though," Glinda said finally. "This whole thing is worrying."

"I know." Betty was quiet for a moment, then said, "One good thing has come from it, though. Gus is taking you to lunch!"

Glinda's cheeks warmed, and she turned away so Betty wouldn't see. She patted at her hair, and said, "He is, isn't he?"

"See? So, something good," Betty said. "And I am sure in a day or two, we will be laughing over the misunderstanding of this whole situation."

"I do hope you are right," Glinda said, trying to ignore the worry that churned and bubbled inside her stomach. It was a shame, really. She was finally going to be alone with Gus, and she might not be able to eat, or think about anything other than this terrible mess that she found herself in.

One thing Glinda didn't want was for Betty to worry. She had her whole life ahead of her. One day, she and Kent would marry, and Betty would be just fine, even without owning this store, if it came to that. The hotel could more than provide for them, and Betty could choose to work there or not, and still be comfortable. Why, she loved running things here so much, perhaps she'd open a small store inside the hotel!

Glinda was about to ask Betty to bag some one-pound sacks of sugar to have at the ready and save time when something caught her eye. She tensed, focusing on the window.

"What is it?" Betty asked, coming alongside her. Then she asked as she craned her neck, "Is that him?"

"Yes," Glinda said flatly, as Mr. Wimer reached her door. She took a deep breath. He wasn't alone. Another man, she presumed his lawyer, walked with him.

"Mrs. Stover," Mr. Wimer said in greeting as he entered her store. The other man glanced around curiously.

"Come to threaten me again?" Glinda asked.

Mr. Wimer sighed. Really, he looked to be an almost kind man, as though what he was saying was difficult for him. However, she found that hard to believe.

"I am Mr. Wimer's lawyer," the other man said as he approached her, though both men stood about eight feet away. "I've got proof that this land, and your store, belong to him. That the Wimers have completed the loan payment that you began and defaulted on."

"And I am in the middle of obtaining proof that I paid off my loan. I've already spoken to the bank," Glinda replied, trying to keep her voice even. "I just need a little more time to reach out to the original banker, the one I made my payments to, as he is no longer here."

"I figure you've had plenty of time, more than long enough, in fact, on my property." Mr. Wimer crossed his arms. "Do I need to get the law involved?"

"Go ahead," Glinda said, heat filling her. "I told you, I'm not interested in selling, and I made my payments. I'm in the right here. You, however, have come in with nothing more than threats. And not a thing will happen before the law approves. Or not."

The lawyer cleared his throat. "Yes, you did make payments. But when they stopped, my client's father bought your loan, along with several others in various towns throughout the state. He resumed payments on this piece of land, and when he passed, the land went to his son. My client."

"What proof do you have that my aunt never paid?" Betty asked, frowning at the man.

"Well—"

"Because if you have it, you've not shown it," Betty said. "All we've heard is talk. And until you do, and in front of the sheriff or the circuit judge to act as a lawful witness, then you are here unwanted, uninvited, and trespassing on her land."

Glinda somehow managed to keep her jaw from dropping, but only just. She'd never imagined such words from Betty, who was always so mild-mannered, and it made her appreciate her hardworking niece all the more.

"So, I'd suggest you leave, and now," Betty added, pointing to the door.

"This isn't over," Mr. Wimer said as he turned and headed toward her door.

"No, it isn't," Glinda agreed.

But even after the door closed, and she saw Gus about to enter, she didn't relax. How could she, when all she'd known, all she'd worked for, was about to be lost? It didn't matter that she'd paid the loan, not if there was no proof of it.

"I'm going to do all I can too, so you don't lose this place," Betty said softly, putting a hand on her arm.

"I appreciate that, dear," Glinda said.

She felt grateful for the words, but that's all they were. She couldn't see any way to get out of the mess she was in. And for a woman who'd faced life head-on, against all the odds of surviving and thriving on her own, that might be the most difficult thing of all to admit.

Chapter 8

"Makes a man want to do something not legal like," Gus grumbled to Billy Madison, as he finished telling him what had been happening with Glinda's store. Eli had asked him to run over some boxes of nails to Billy, who was mending the fence along their shared land, and he took advantage of the moment to update the man.

"Poor woman," Billy said, his usually cheerful expression and tone sour. "Sounds suspicious to me."

"I think so too," Gus answered.

Billy took his hat off, wiped his brow, and put it back on. He glanced around to make sure the hired workers weren't listening in. "Wonder if she's asked Kent to watch the man. After all, it's his hotel the guy is at."

"True," Gus mused. "Was wondering when yer friend Ryan Lundy was coming back to town. Might be he could find something out."

Ryan was a fine tracker. Had recovered more gold than Gus had ever witnessed in his lifetime at once, and right here in town too. Had also saved Billy's wife's best friend from a terrible situation. As sometimes happened, at leastways around here, they fell in love. However, Ryan had been away for a few weeks now on a job. Gus bet Callie was pining something awful. That happened with young love. Old too, in his case.

"Don't know," Billy said. "But we can handle this one." He added, "With you here, this town hasn't ever been without the help it needs."

"True enough," Gus said, trying not to let his chest puff up too much. It was honest fact, though, there wasn't much he didn't or couldn't do to help folks in town.

'Course, it didn't need mentioning how he'd pretty much single-handedly run Hannah's place for a while, but he'd also helped repair the church roof when a storm came through, did odd jobs for Madge over at the diner, free of charge except for a slice of her pie, and then there were all of those times he'd helped Glinda in her store. Those heavy sacks didn't lift themselves.

Having been here nearly since the formation of the town, he felt like one of the founders. "I think I'd like to talk to the man myself." He hooked his fingers at his waist.

"See what he's all about with my own eyes. Hoping to see him today."

"Want a little backup?" Billy asked.

Gus considered the offer. He imagined himself swaggering into the hotel, the finest gunslingers that ever lived behind him, his arms crossed, that special kinda look he saved for when he was especially perturbed. He'd scowl a little. Make his brows lower. It wasn't unappealing, this idea of Billy's.

He rubbed at his chin a moment, then shook his head. That wasn't him. No matter how much fun it sounded. "Naw, got my own kind of persuasion," Gus said. "Perk of being old is don't nobody think you're a threat. But ain't nobody taking away Glinda's store. They'll have to get through me first, and I ain't moving."

"You're a good man," Billy said, thumping him on the shoulder. "She's lucky to have you around."

"Hope she feels the same," Gus grunted, refusing to rub at his shoulder where it was feeling a mite sore after the clap. "Now, if you'll excuse me. Me and Glinda got us a lunch appointment."

He waved to the gunslinger and went to the hitching post. He loosened the mare's reins and whistled as he rode to town. It was going to be fine weather today. His knee told him so. Sunshine, no rain on the horizon, but a chilly breeze to keep it from getting hot and to signal cooler days ahead.

As he rode into the town, a figure caught his eye, and he rode up to them. "Well, well," Gus said as he stopped the horse and removed his hat. "You find your way with my directions?"

The young woman he'd helped a few days prior gave him a nervous smile. Poor woman. Obviously intimidated by him. He'd have to try harder not to look threatening. Was good for the likes of the man trying to take over Glinda's store, but not for innocent young ladies. He put his hat back on.

"Yes, your...precise directions were very helpful," the woman answered.

"Happy to have been of service," Gus told her. "You ever get lost again, just ask for Old Gus. Better than a map!"

"Uh, yes, I thank you," the woman said and hurried away.

Gus nodded after her, then continued on. Since he and Glinda were going to have lunch, he thought he'd board the mare at the livery. A few moments later, he was striding over to the general store.

Two men came out, both looking agitated. Gus considered going after them, but didn't want to upset anything, if Glinda had just sent them on their way. As he walked inside, he asked, "That the feller's lawyer?"

"Yes," Glinda said, approaching him. Her lips were pressed together.

"I'm glad you're here," Betty told him from behind the counter. "Take as long as you like, Aunt Glinda. Maybe a change of scenery will make you feel better."

"What will make me feel better," Glinda said, as she reached for her hat and put it on, "is to have that man and his lawyer leave, and never come back."

"Fill me in as we walk over," Gus told her.

Glinda did just that, and Gus found his frown deepening. "Ain't right," he said. "Not at all, but don't you worry none. We're looking into it too."

"I'm trying hard not to worry," Glinda said with a heavy sigh. "Everyone keeps telling me not to, but Gus, this is my livelihood! It's my everything. How can I not worry?"

How he wanted to tell her it wasn't her everything. That she had him. Could rely on him. But Gus knew what she meant. Instead, he held open the diner door, and waited for her to walk in before he said, "I might not know how it's going to turn out just yet, but I know it will be just fine in the end."

"Hello and welcome. Where do you two want to sit?" a woman, perhaps in her early thirties, asked as she walked toward them.

"Anywhere, Joy, thank you," Glinda said.

"How about this nice window spot?" Joy answered, leading them to a table. "We've got a vegetable stew and cornbread or ham steaks, green beans, and biscuits. For dessert, there is peach cobbler or pumpkin pie."

"What'll you have?" Gus asked Glinda.

"I'll do the stew and the cobbler," Glinda said. "With some tea, please."

"Gus?" Joy asked.

"I'd like me the ham, the pie, and some coffee," he told her.

With a short nod, Joy was off to the kitchen, where he knew in just a moment, she'd have the food set before them. Madge ran a good diner, and she, and her cook, Lisa, had things down to a tight routine. With Joy here helping with the serving, a body never waited long at all.

Sure enough, their meal came right out, and Gus took a long drink from his mug. As he sat it down and took his first bite, he couldn't help but wish that he knew exactly what to say to make things right for Glinda. He hated to see her this way.

"The most difficult part of this all," Glinda said, almost as if she'd been talking for a time before leading into that, "is how those men have made me feel as though I'm a criminal!"

"We both know you ain't," Gus told her. "Everybody else here in town knows it too."

"I hope so," Glinda murmured. After a bite of stew, she added, "Sometimes folks say something, but after a time of it brewing around in your head, you start to second-guess your own thoughts and wonder if they are right."

"In this case," Gus told her, "it's not true."

They ate quietly for a moment, but Gus's mind was spinning. "You heard from the banker yet?" he asked.

"No, I've not. I know it might be too soon for a reply, but I thought I'd stop over there after we eat."

"Mind some company?" Gus asked.

"I'd be right grateful for it," Glinda said. "Gus, I...I don't know what I'd do without you. Not just right now, but all the other times you've helped me."

Gus felt his face heat up something fierce, and looked down at a biscuit, making more work out of buttering it than strictly necessary. "Shucks, just being a good friend is all," he said. Then he could have kicked himself. Why had he said that? Wouldn't this have been a better time to tell her how he really felt about her?

"You've done far more than that," Glinda said softly. "When I think about how you looked after me and Betty when the store was broken into and we had all that mess in town, the times that you've done errands for me, carried something heavy, even just listened to all my worries. It sure means a lot to me. I can't imagine my life without you in it. Maybe...maybe that's also part of my worry with all this. If I...if I have to leave."

This was it. This was his opening. But just as Gus opened his mouth to tell Glinda how he really felt, Joy came up and plopped down their desserts. "Here you are," she told them. "More to drink?" Before either could answer, she'd taken away their cups and returned just as quickly with them filled again.

The mood was different now. The place was filling up, Gus realized as he looked around. Another time, perhaps. There was no way he could say what he wanted with this many people around.

He finished his meal, then slid his pie toward him. "Sure do love this pie in the fall," he said.

"Do you remember when Mrs. Blackstone made one a few years ago for a church potluck, and the Smiths' dog snatched it off the table?" Glinda asked, laughing.

"Sure do! Was right sad," Gus answered with a chuckle. "Coulda waited till I got my slice."

Their conversation became lighter, as they reminisced about the years they'd been there, and some of the things they'd done. An hour later as they left the diner, both smiling and laughing, Gus felt that ache again in his chest.

He didn't want to be without her any longer. He wanted to be there, by her side, when she had troubles, like these. He wanted to be the one to help her with all the things she needed doing, laughing over stories, reminiscing, and hoped he'd find the words to tell her so before it was too late.

Despite him telling her not to worry, the simple fact remained that if this Wimer feller did take over her land and business and tore it all down, Glinda might leave. And he wouldn't have an excuse to follow her.

The thought chilled Gus, and he realized one more thing. If that were the case, if he lost out on seeing Glinda's beautiful face every day, he wouldn't be long for this world. He'd die of heartbreak first.

Chapter 9

For just a few moments, as she and Gus had laughed and found themselves in the past, she had forgotten. Forgotten about her store. Forgotten about Mr. Wimer. Forgotten that she was in a terrible situation that, despite everyone reassuring her all would be well, didn't seem likely.

Gus seemed to sense that and hesitantly offered his arm. Glinda slid her hand onto it, taking comfort in his nearness, and wondering at those little twinkles of light that seemed to be bursting inside of her stomach. She'd never really felt them before, but they were quite delightful, and now that she'd had them, she wanted them to never go away.

They walked toward the bank, neither of them saying anything. It was too short of a walk, and they had to separate to go inside. Glinda wished it had been a few miles away. She'd have happily walked hours just to continue being that close to him. When they stepped apart, the lovely little sparkles in her stomach faded in a most disappointing way.

As they walked inside the bank, Glinda was relieved to see it vacant, except for a young teller, and Mr. Logan sitting at his desk. He glanced up, and then stood, offering a wan smile.

"I am sure I know why you are here," he said quietly, "but I regret to inform you I have no news as of yet."

"None at all?" Glinda nearly cried out. "What of the message you sent?"

"Here, sit," Mr. Logan said, gesturing to two chairs in front of his desk. Once they had, he returned to his, and leaned forward slightly, elbows on his desktop. "I did send the message, inquiring where the former bank manager, Mr. Thomas, had moved to. I was told that he and his wife had gone to Dixonburg, for him to be the bank manager there. That's a few hours away. Immediately, I sent another message to that town."

"That's wonderful," Glinda answered, almost breathless. "We've found him!"

The banker held up his hand. "It's a small thing, which is more than we had, yes. However, there's been no reply. Now, it could simply be that the bank has not had time to answer, or it could be that they have no answer to give. Mr.

Thomas might not live there any longer. He might never have moved there and taken the position."

"If that's the case, there must be something more you can do!" Glinda said, ashamed she was nearly begging. "Have you looked again for the missing ledgers?"

"I have," Mr. Logan assured her, looking regretful. "I'm so sorry, Mrs. Stover. I've been unable to find them."

Glinda nodded, and looked at her hands clasped in her lap. What else was there to try? Normally, she was a clear-headed woman. Able to think up solutions to most any problem. Why, she'd been doing that her whole life, as she'd had to manage on her own. This was just another time she needed to, so why was she struggling to know the next step?

Glinda rose suddenly. "Thank you, Mr. Logan. I will send my own message there, and perhaps one of us will get an answer."

"Of course. I'm sorry I can't be of more help," Mr. Logan said.

She could see in his eyes he did feel badly, and forced a smile. "I understand you are doing all you can," she told him.

Gus followed her outside and studied her for a moment. She'd known him long enough to tell he had something on his mind. Before she could offer a penny for his thoughts, he spoke.

"There's no need for you to send a message," Gus told her suddenly.

"What do you mean?" Glinda asked. "Of course I must. Perhaps the first didn't get through."

He shook his head. "What I mean is, I'll be your message. Messenger. Whatever. I'm riding over to Dixonburg just as soon as I let Hannah and Eli know."

Glinda's hands flew to her mouth. "Oh no! I won't let you do that! It might be a wasted trip, and it's so far!"

"Ain't nothing wasted when it comes to you," Gus told her firmly.

His words made her feel tongue-tied, and she stuttered for a moment, finally saying, "This is my problem, my worry. I don't want to be a bother to anyone."

"I hope I ain't just anyone," Gus told her, suddenly reaching for one of her hands, "and the last thing you are, Glinda Louise Stover, is a bother. You're special. I might be a little bold in saying this, but I'd do anything for you. Anything at all if it would bring you happiness."

"Gus," she whispered, her eyes locked on his. "I..."

But nothing more came. Her words had frozen, and the gentle pressure on her hand seemed to be all she could focus on.

"I'll be back soon as I can, and I hope with some good news," Gus told her. "I aim to track down that banker man, Mr. Thomas, and if he ain't there, I'll find out where he is."

"Promise me you'll be safe," Glinda pleaded, placing a hand on his arm. "If anything were to happen to you..." She swallowed past the cotton in her mouth and softly said, "You aren't just anyone, Gus. You're...you're real special to me, too. And I..."

Tears, hot, fat, and embarrassing started to roll down her cheeks. She dropped her gaze, not wanting to see Gus's reaction. A man didn't like a woman who got emotional.

But to her surprise, he reached out, raised her chin up, and looked at her with surprise. "No woman ever cried over me before," he said, wonder in his voice. He gently wiped at her cheeks with his hand, and said, "My knee tells me it's a fine day for travel. Don't you worry none about me. But I don't want you by yourself."

"Betty will be nearby," Glinda promised him. "And Kent has offered to come if we need him."

"Good man." Gus nodded.

"Almost as good as you," Glinda said shyly.

He ducked his head. "I better git while it's daylight," Gus told her. "But reckon we can do this again? The diner? Maybe a walk after? Me...holding on to you?"

"I'd like that very much," Glinda said softly. She reluctantly stepped back, and he nodded again, a little nervously. She could see his Adam's apple bobbing.

"Right. See you soon," he said, and turned toward the livery, moving at a quick pace.

Glinda watched as he went inside the building and emerged a moment later on his horse, and then, impulsively, blew him a kiss. His whole face lit up, and he grinned, caught it, and rode away at a fast canter.

Dust swirled behind him, and Glinda stood in the spot he'd left her, until she could no longer see him. As she turned back to her store, she felt a fleeting drop of hope flicker. Maybe he could help. It could be all wasn't at a loss. Not her store, and—her cheeks flamed—not her chance for romance.

But as she started to open her store door, she saw Mr. Wimer and his lawyer standing in front of the hotel, a large paper unrolled between them, nodding and pointing in her direction.

Taking a deep breath, she steeled herself and walked inside her building. For as long as she could hold on to the store, she would. She might be terrified and about to collapse under the stress, but she wasn't going to let either of those men see it. This place was still hers, and she aimed to keep it that way.

Chapter 10

While Gus might not admit it to anyone else, as he rode away from Glinda, her wide eyes watching him, he felt a little like a hero. It felt good, too. Was this what the younger fellers felt like, helping protect the women they had? Gus just hoped he'd be able to help his.

While the banker had been talking, Gus had been thinking. As soon as he heard the town name Dixonburg, he recollected that the banker's sister's husband's cousin's nephew was one of the farmhands who'd been there at Hannah's place back before Carson bought them all out.

Should be right easy to track the family down, even if Mr. Thomas wasn't still there because there might still be some kin nearby. As much as he wanted to go straight away and not waste any daylight, it wouldn't be the responsible thing, leaving Hannah and Eli without knowing his whereabouts, and from his own lips.

Lips...

Glinda had blown him a kiss. Did that mean she might be willing to give him one for real one day?

A silly grin formed on his face, and if he hadn't been in such a hurry, Gus might have allowed himself to replay that moment a few more times.

But daylight was fading and there was a lot to do.

As Gus rode up, maybe a little quicker than usual, Hannah came out through the kitchen door, her arms crossed. She smiled at him and shook her head.

"You look like you're up to no good," she told him as she leaned against the doorframe.

That made him laugh. "I'm always up to no good. Otherwise, what's the fun?" He winked as he got out of the wagon. "Afore you ask, I didn't get the cornmeal. I might have a way to help Glinda, and I'm heading there now."

"Where's there?" Hannah asked him.

"Over to Dixonburg, where the man who used to be banker could be."

"All alone? Are you sure?" Hannah worried at her bottom lip before saying, "That's such a long way."

"Sure, I'm sure. It's harmless. You'll see. I'll be much faster there and back than sending another letter and waiting around for an answer."

"Do you want to wait for Eli to return?" Hannah asked. "Or—"

"Can't. Got me a feeling I got to go now. I can't let Glinda's hard work be for nothing. If I can help her, I will. Don't you worry none. Thinking I'll be home late tonight or tomorrow afternoon."

"I see I can't make you change your mind. I understand, and it's for a noble cause. But be careful, Gus," Hannah said softly. "I don't know what I'd do if something happened to you. I suspect a good number of others feel just the same. You're family. Remember that."

He swallowed the lump that formed as he undid the last of the harness connecting the horse to the wagon, bending his head so she wouldn't see. "Don't you worry about me," he assured her. "Leaving now, so's I get back sooner."

As he hurried off for the second time in the last hour, Gus couldn't think about how grateful he was for friends so good they were like family. He hoped he was telling Hannah the truth about when he'd be back. More importantly, he hoped that he'd be returning with whatever Glinda needed to save her livelihood.

His mare's hooves were rhythmic, and he let them lull him as he rode across the open roads and fields to Dixonburg. Meanwhile, he tried to put together a plan.

"First thing is finding the man or his kin," Gus worked out.

He thought back to his interactions with Mr. Thomas over the years, trying to remember the man. There hadn't been too many. He'd been a small man, as Gus remembered. Eyes a little too close together. Not much on top. Unlike him. No, the Lord had blessed him with an enviable and thick head of hair, and Gus might have been just a little more proud than he ought to be, but a man deserved to take a little pride in his appearance, didn't he?

One thing he did keep turning over in his mind was why, if a message had been sent, did the former Red Ridge banker not reply? The only thing he could think of was either the man hadn't gotten the message, wasn't still living, or else was trying to hide. The last two didn't bode well for Glinda if that were the case.

Knowing Gavin, he'd sent a message as well to the town sheriff, but chances were it would still be faster with him paying a visit. Gus glanced down at his mare. She was enjoying the easy run. Eli had gifted her to him a few months back. The best horse he'd ever called his own.

"*The man who runs Hannah's ranch and protected her from harm for so long deserves nothing less,*" Eli had told him, quite properly ignoring the tears that had escaped Gus's eyes. He was getting mighty sentimental in his old age.

He was glad to have the horse, though. She'd likely be able to make it the whole way with just a single stop.

A flicker of movement caught Gus's eye and he turned his head. Whatever red flash he'd seen wasn't there now. He kept riding, but it was hard now to ignore the prickle of unease that crept up on him.

There was relief in his bones when eventually Dixonburg appeared up over a rise. He found the livery, paid well for the mare to be taken care of, and then asked, "You know a man by the last name of Thomas? Used to be a banker? Might still be?"

The man he asked thought a moment, then shook his head. "Don't think so," he said. "That's not our banker's name. Could ask at the general store. The post office is there too, so they know everybody."

Gus nodded his thanks, and spent the next two hours asking one person and then the next. From the general store to the diner to the tailor, because the man might have a fancy suit, to the blacksmith, and just about everyone in between. Finally, he stopped in front of the bank. "Should have started here, reckon maybe," he said. "Don't know why I didn't."

Gus reached for the door and froze. A flicker of red caught his attention, but when he glanced over, there wasn't anyone there. Again.

But not too far away, a bush was swaying a little, and Gus felt sure he could see a hint of color inside it. Unnatural color. There wasn't red on a shrub like that.

Was he being followed? And by who? Gus walked past the bank and took himself over to the town spring, where he took a long time drinking from the tin cup hooked to a chain. His eyes went every which way, but he didn't see anyone. Only sensed them. The prickles all up and down his spine were warning him something fierce that he wasn't alone.

"Wonder if it's that lawyer man," Gus muttered. "Or just a body trying to thieve from an old man."

Didn't matter. Whoever it was, he wasn't going to let them—or anything else—keep him from what he needed to do. Which was help Glinda.

Gus straightened from his stoop, took a last long look, and then headed toward the bush. He'd take the fellow by surprise, that's what he'd do.

But when he suddenly leaped onto the brush, parting it with his arms, there was nothing inside but a recently bent branch that snagged on his shirt sleeve.

Gus squinted and looked around. Had he imagined it? Had it been a bird? Sure hadn't looked like one, and he didn't think no songbird would be causing those prickles like he'd had.

It was tempting to look around some more, see if he could spot what wasn't right, but he couldn't dally. If someone was going to stop him, they'd either do it before he got there to the bank or after. Either way, he'd be ready.

He took one last look around him, strode to the bank, and hoped Glinda's answer was waiting inside.

Chapter 11

"Can I get you anything else, Mrs. Blackstone?" Glinda asked, as she began to load the pastor's wife's basket with the goods she'd come in to purchase. Her elbow accidentally knocked over a tin of sweets, and as she picked it up and examined it for damage, she said, "I do apologize. How clumsy of me."

"I do that all the time," Mrs. Blackstone replied, helping to load the basket. "And no, there's nothing more Horace or I need. However," she hesitated, then lowered her voice, "I do hope that I'm not stepping out of place, but I wanted you to know that we support you. We both know what kind of a woman you are—one of the highest moral character, and we have been praying for a quick resolution for your situation."

It was all that Glinda could do to remain with her shoulders high, when they wanted to slump in defeat. The pastor's wife didn't have a drop of gossiping tendencies or ill intent in her veins, but this meant word had been stretching further about the difficulties she was facing far faster than she'd hoped.

As if she sensed the worried thoughts racing through Glinda's mind, Mrs. Blackstone added, "Mirabelle told us, but I assure you, it's not common knowledge."

She nodded, allowing that spark of relief to latch on. That made sense. Mirabelle would have learned it from Billy, the sheriff's close friend, and one of the town's protectors. "I appreciate that," she said, giving in to the wobble that seemed to lurk just beneath the surface of her speech these days.

That morning, she'd stared into the mirror and wondered at the frightened woman before her. Where was the confident Glinda Stover, unafraid and unwilling to accept defeat in any situation? Who stared back was a woman who seemed to have aged a lifetime in just a few days, with dark circles under her eyes and a bone-weary expression on her face.

"If there is a way that we can help, I expect you to tell us," the pastor's wife continued. "Not because of pastoral duty, but because of friendship, and because you are important to our town. We need you."

Tears came from nowhere and slid down Glinda's cheeks as she nodded. "I will. That means more to me than you can know."

The pastor's wife simply squeezed her hand, then turned away, picking up her basket to situate it on one arm while walking toward the shop door. Glinda watched her leave, and glanced around the store. She'd always taken such pride in the ownership of it, and these last few exceptionally trying days hadn't dampened that whatsoever.

Her windows weren't just clean, they nearly sparkled. Store displays weren't put out haphazardly or without thought to get as many items before her customers as possible. No, they were efficient, artistic, designed to draw the eye, make it easier for anyone browsing or buying. Of course, if it improved sales, that was just a little bonus.

Everything was done with a purpose, with consideration behind it, and oh how it had paid off. She had not only something she was incredibly proud of, built from almost nothing, but she had customers who appreciated her store. Appreciated the care and quality and her honesty.

She couldn't lose the store. It was all she had, and she was far too old to simply start over again. It would also be much harder in an area nearby, as by then the story would be out and people might suspect her of wrongdoing, even if that couldn't be any further from the truth. Besides, what would there be to start over with?

And then there was Gus...

Betty came from the back of the store, a few sticks of wood in her hands that she stacked in the basket by the stove. "I wonder if that will be enough for the rest of today and tomorrow," she said, eyeing it critically.

"It will be plenty," Glinda said. Then, almost bitingly, she added, "However, I'll burn it all in spite if that man takes my store. Let him fund his own supply. Why, I might even consider letting the store go up in flames, so he doesn't sell off the shelves and lumber."

Her niece gasped. "Aunt Glinda! No!"

"You are right. I wouldn't do that," Glinda said with a sigh. "Only because I couldn't bear to watch my hard work in flames. It will be bad enough if it's torn down, and a resort put in."

"That won't happen," Betty said fiercely, crossing her arms over her chest.

"It will, unless I do something," Glinda said. "I just don't know what that something is. How can I go against the proof that someone else owns my store?"

"We still need to see that evidence," Betty reminded her.

"Yes, I know. And I also know that I am not entirely in this fight by myself. However, in the end, the store's successes or its losses fall entirely on my shoulders."

Betty bit her lip, then asked slowly, "Aunt Glinda, you don't suppose this is some sort of a false story, do you? A scheme to take advantage of you?"

"What do you mean?" Glinda asked.

"Well, forgive me for being blunt, but you are a woman in her later years living here alone. At least, you were until recently. I don't know the value of the land nor the store, but one can reasonably assume that you run a successful business, one that pays for itself, for quality goods, an employee, and you have enough to be comfortable in your life."

"That's all true," Glinda agreed.

Betty began to tick off on her fingers. "You are also unmarried, not planning to wed, and have little family. Your son, the most likely to inherit your property, doesn't live nearby, and has no interest in the store. With his distance, that also means he doesn't know all that goes on with you."

"That is also true," Glinda said. "And you are suspecting that someone is aware of this, and has perhaps gotten the idea they can take my land without any fight?"

"I don't know," Betty admitted. "But it's a possibility. Kent was telling me how dangerous it can be for an older woman. They are often seen as easy prey."

"He would know," Glinda mused, though she didn't mean it in any way other than fact. His past was his past, and he'd atoned for it.

After a moment of mulling over the idea, she shrugged. "I don't know. This doesn't feel like that. For one thing, if it were some sort of attempt to cheat me, wouldn't Mr. Wimer or his lawyer have tried to flatter me? Get closer to me to see just what I have? Neither has, and both claim to have proof, and also have a good story of how they obtained the land."

"That's true. It just doesn't seem right that your loan could be transferred to payments made by someone else," Betty said. "Is that legal?"

"I admit, that isn't something I know." Glinda frowned. "I wonder how much they paid. How much I have. If I could give them something to make them just...go away."

"Don't do that," Betty begged. "It might make the situation worse."

"But it also might be the answer," Glinda said. "Will you watch the store for me?"

Betty's face was full of trepidation, but she nodded.

Without even bothering to remove her apron or get her hat, Glinda marched out of the store, the determination—and foolishness—of her idea filling her. It wasn't much of a plan; in fact, it wasn't a plan at all. It was a bribe. A last hope. A desperate attempt.

But it was also all that she had, and she had to do it.

When she opened the bank door, Mr. Logan rose upon seeing her. Before he could greet her, Glinda pushed the words past her tight chest and quivering heart and said,

"I'd like to know how much money I have. Every cent, please."

"Of course. One moment." The bank manager picked up a thick ledger from his desk and opened the maroon cover. He turned a few pages and then nodded to himself, picked up a pencil, and wrote carefully on a scrap piece of paper. "Here you are."

Glinda glanced at it. The numbers seemed right. Perhaps even a little more than she'd thought. "Thank you," she said, and turned on her heel before he could ask any questions.

She was already starting to lose her nerve and wanted to hurry and make the offer before her practical side learned what her impulsive one was doing.

Not much later, she was in the hotel lobby, trying not to impatiently tap her second-best boots against the polished wooden floor. The desk manager had promised to fetch Mr. Wimer. Glinda just hadn't thought the waiting would be so unbearable.

"Mrs. Stover?"

She turned at the sound of her name. Mr. Wimer was there, staring at her in surprise. "Yes. I've come to make an offer," she said, thrusting a piece of paper at him. "Every cent I own. It's all there at the bank. If you leave town and never bother me or my shop again, it's yours."

The man looked at the paper and then shook his head, folded it, and returned it to her. "I'm sorry. I am sure that to a woman such as yourself, this is a large amount. To me, however, it is not. I can make triple this in the first six months alone with a resort. Why would I settle for so little, when I could have far more?"

"To do the right thing," she answered through gritted teeth.

"The right thing would have been to repay your loan," he replied neutrally.

"I did!" she exclaimed.

Mr. Wimer pinched the bridge of his nose. "Now, look, Mrs. Stover. I'm not a bad person. I'm not unreasonable. I'm a businessman who prides himself on honesty. But I have proof that this land is mine. While I'm sorry for whatever might have happened to cause you to default on your obligation, legally, the land and anything on it is mine. I don't want your money, I want the land. Additionally, your being here and making me this offer doesn't make you look good."

It hadn't worked. Glinda didn't know why she'd hoped it would. Of course he wouldn't want her money. It was a good deal, to her, but for a man such as him, perhaps it was an insult, and had made things more difficult for her. She wished that she hadn't approached him. It might have been better to get the evidence first. Now, it looked as though she were trying to buy him off. That could be incriminating.

"I'd like to see this proof you keep talking about," Glinda said. She raised her chin a little defiantly. "I deserve to see it."

"In due time, Mrs. Stover," the man said. "My lawyer has it, and we plan to show it to the sheriff and the judge at the same time. Word has been sent, asking the man to come here. I plan to do things legally—even if you didn't."

Glinda gasped in a combination of mortification and anger, then stood there uncertain of her next steps. She'd never felt so helpless or alone in all her life. There was no one to talk to, no one to advise her. No one to do more than to tell her not to worry. And what good was that? Glinda bowed her head and left wordlessly.

The sound of her heart shattering echoed in her ears, while the weight in her legs made her sway. She was acutely aware that Mr. Wimer's eyes followed her, and that, to him, she must appear defeated. But if Glinda Stover was anything, it wouldn't be defeated. Just he wait.

Chapter 12

This bank was similar to every other one Gus had ever walked inside. A protected area behind bars, pleasant-looking employees, and that smell that always set his nose to tickling. It made him curious. Was that a requirement in a bank? It needed to make a body's nose itch something fierce?

"May I help you, sir?" a young woman asked, looking up at him with a smile.

"Sure can." He hooked his thumbs into his belt. "I'd like to see your bank manager," Gus told her.

"That would be me, sir," came the answer, as a man a little older than Eli appeared. "How may I be of help?"

"Howdy. Looking for a man named Mr. Thomas. Used to be the banker at Red Ridge. We got us a problem that happened when he was running the place and need his help to figure it out."

The bank manager pressed his lips together. "Why doesn't that surprise me? I'm Todd McGuire. I've been here for a while now. However, I'm afraid you've come all this way for nothing."

"That so?" Gus asked. His eyes narrowed slightly. Was the man lying?

"Yes. Mr. Thomas took sick with fever a few years ago. When he died, his wife up and moved along with the rest of her family who had been here. Don't know where. I couldn't tell you much about her. Him, though...he was a dishonest man, I can tell you that. That's why I suspect they all left. Whatever trouble you have down your way, he may have caused, but I'm not sure I have a way to help you."

The news hit him hard, and Gus felt any hope he'd had leave. He'd been so sure there would be an answer. Was this why no one from the town had replied? Mr. Thomas was dead?

"An honest woman is in danger of losing all she has," Gus said. "Me getting proof she done paid her loan in full to Mr. Thomas was why we needed him."

The banker grimaced. "Shouldn't speak ill of the dead, but seemed with him, when you were making your payments, they didn't always get there."

"Don't reckon you know anything about a loan to a Glinda Stover?" Gus asked.

"I'm afraid not," the banker said, a touch of sympathy in his voice. "I know Mr. Thomas was dishonest in his profession when he was here; however, I don't know anything about him or his other clients beyond this town. All I have is the reason he was replaced, which was that when payments were made to him, they weren't always given to the bank."

Gus pushed his lips out while he thought for a moment. "And you got you some evidence about that?"

"I do," Mr. McGuire said. "The bank kept all the records, just in case they were needed later. I have statements from a good number of people, including the sheriff, his deputy, the judge."

"Just wish we had the same," Gus said, looking down at his worn boots. "Glinda done spent her whole life in Red Ridge, built her store ground up, and a man's threatening to take it, saying it's him who paid the loan, not her, even though she knows she paid off the bank. Wonder if that means he was taken in by this Mr. Thomas too."

Mr. McGuire shook his head. "That does sound like a terrible situation. I don't know what good it will do, but I could share what information I have in a letter with the sheriff and the circuit rider judge. I can't give specifics, like names and amounts to you, I'm afraid, only that I possess knowledge of his wrongdoings, but they could ask for it, as representatives of the law, and I'd be able to supply it."

"It's something, which is better than nothing," Gus said. "I'd thankee kindly, if you would. I know our sheriff will sure as sure follow up with you."

"Give me just a few moments," the banker said. He pointed to a few chairs across the bank lobby. "Why don't you sit while I work on that?"

Gus nodded, and went over to the chairs. They were soft and covered in such a fancy fabric, he almost felt afraid to sit on them. Give him a hard wooden chair or a stool any day. Maybe a cushion with it. That he felt better around. He was a simple man. Always had been. As the thought came to him, he wondered what kind of chairs Glinda had in her home. Worn and comfortable? Fussy?

Gingerly, he sat, hoping he wouldn't get one dirty, and touched his shirt pocket. Inside lay a scrap of a handkerchief. That's all it was now, it was so old, but once, he'd cut his finger and Glinda had happened upon him.

When she'd seen his injury, she'd tied the bit of dainty around his finger. He'd offered to return it, but she'd told him to keep it. So he had. The hankie had stayed by his side ever since, though the faint scent of violet water she wore had long faded. That had been...almost ten years ago now?

Funny how he'd held her in his heart so fiercely, and for so long, yet, he'd never been able to bring himself to tell her. Gus swallowed hard as his mind wandered over the many times he'd wanted to talk to Glinda but hadn't let himself.

Though the circumstances weren't favorable right now, they had done one thing, and that was give him reason to spend more time with her. And then she'd blown him that kiss...

"Sir?"

His head snapped up, and his body joined a second later, coming up out of the chair. "That for me?"

The banker was holding out an envelope. "Yes. I've included the bank address, and my personal information for anyone who needs to contact me."

"I appreciate your help," Gus said, sticking out his hand.

As they shook, Mr. McGuire said, "I wish you the best in what you are trying to accomplish."

Gus nodded his thanks and left. He started toward the livery, but a flicker of red from the corner of his eye made him hesitate. What if he rode out of town with what he needed to help Glinda, and it was taken from him? He'd never forgive himself.

He glanced around looking for the sheriff's office and spotted it not too far away. The door was closed, and the open window had no movement beyond. The man might not be there. Gus looked at it, considering. He could walk over, see for himself. The smart thing would be to let the man know of his suspicion.

However, he hadn't always done the smart things in life. Too often, they hadn't panned out. Sometimes, a man had to do the thing his gut was telling him. The thing he was sure would get the job done.

And right now, his gut was telling him to take care of this problem himself. He may be on his own, but he wasn't helpless. There might not be much time to make up a plan, but that was all right. He wasn't going down without a fight, and if he got into one, he planned to do whatever it took to win.

Hoping that the thudding of his heart wasn't too loud, Gus turned the corner. Time to set a trap. Glinda depended on him. He just hoped he had it in him.

Chapter 13

Somehow, Glinda made it back to her store, shoulders back, head held high. But the moment the door closed behind her, her eyes did as well, and her legs felt weak. She gripped the doorframe.

"Aunt Glinda!" Betty gasped, rushing toward her.

The sheriff's wife, Winnie, and her sister, Lily, were there shopping, and also started moving toward her in alarm.

"I'm fine," Glinda said, holding up a hand to stall them, but it wasn't the truth. Her pulse was too quick, and it was difficult to draw in a breath through her tight chest. There was a sharp cramp. She wanted to ask Betty to get the doctor, but the words wouldn't form. Suddenly, she felt both blazingly hot and icy cold.

She'd never felt such a thing before, and her constitution was quite good, so Glinda had no idea what was wrong. Surely she wasn't sick. It must just be the stress. Panic? But even as she tried to reason what could be the matter with her, Glinda felt her mind moving sluggishly.

Glinda forced herself to look at Betty. Her niece's mouth was moving, and it was obvious she was talking, but the rushing noise in Glinda's ears was so loud, she couldn't make out anything. She tried to step toward her niece, but the moment she was no longer supported by the door, Glinda wobbled and then fell.

Her head struck the corner of a low table she'd been intending to move closer to the large plate-glass window, and the last thing Glinda remembered was the incredible pain, something warm trickling down her head, and the scream that tore from Betty's lips.

***

"Don't you dare move from this bed," an unfamiliar male voice said.

Glinda froze, cracked her eyes open, and then blinked up into the doctor's stern face. "Doctor, I am—"

"Quite lucky you didn't do more than gash the back of your head," he said. "Your niece told me to scold you, so I shall. You gave her, Winnie, and Lily a terrible fright."

"Not you?" Glinda asked, gingerly bringing a hand to the sore spot on her scalp.

"I'm in love with a woman whose brother is a gunslinger," Dr. Rycroft answered wryly. "There's not much to me that's scarier. If I misstep…" His eyes widened as he shook his head and winced.

She chuckled along with him a second later. After he'd saved the town from the sweeping illness, and become more comfortable in his new home, he'd seemed to relax slightly and show his personality. The doctor was both a brilliant man, and one who cared deeply for his patients in the town.

"They are good men," she finally answered, then closed her eyes again. "I can't believe I fell."

"Betty told me you've been under a good deal of stress," the doctor said gently, as his cool fingers found the pulse point of her wrist. "I suspect it was that which caused it."

"Perhaps it was," Glinda sighed. "Things are…difficult just now."

"Unless you want something like that happening again, I suggest that you try to remain calm," he told her. "Relaxed. Do less."

"How can I?" she protested, trying to sit up. At his stern finger wag, she lay back down. "I'm trying to save my store."

"I understand, and you have my deepest sympathies for your situation. It's not one I'd wish on anyone. However, what if this happens again? Worse, when you are alone? This time, the laceration is shallow. It will be sore more than it will be worrying. But next time?"

He was right. As much as she hated to admit it, the doctor had a point. But she still needed to figure out what to do about Mr. Wimer and his lawyer. Being lazy abed wouldn't help her do that.

Dr. Rycroft sighed and snapped his doctor's bag closed. "I can see in your eyes you are planning to do as you wish, but please rest. If not for yourself, then for your friends and family who are concerned about you. Even if it's just for today, it would do you good."

"I will," Glinda promised, though the moment the door was shut behind her, she slowly worked herself to sitting with only a little difficulty. The ache in her head was the worst of it, she was sure.

Her door opened just then, and Betty's disapproving expression met her eyes. "What do you think you are doing?" her niece asked. "I knew he wouldn't scold you properly!"

"He did, but I'm sitting up," Glinda said firmly. "I've a store to run, and—"

"And I can do it splendidly," Betty retorted. "You need to—"

"Fine," Glinda sighed. Her head hurt too much to argue. "But just for today."

Her niece nodded approvingly, and left. Glinda let herself doze, and a few times startled awake, something of importance just at the edge of her consciousness. She just didn't know what. A thought kept niggling at the back of her mind, never quite coming to the surface. She knew it was urgent, but couldn't grasp what it was.

She drifted away to sleep again. This time, she had that feeling one sometimes did of working, though she knew she wasn't awake.

Glinda tallied up order after order at her store. "Here you are," she said to each customer, writing down the order total on a receipt and keeping a copy for herself and giving one to them. Over and over, she found herself going through the motion.

Order, receipt, copy. Order, receipt, copy. Order, receipt—

Suddenly, her eyes flew open. This time she was fully awake. "My receipts! My copy!"

Glinda struggled to get out of bed. As a business owner herself, she knew the importance of good receipts. Hers were always precise and detailed. A copy for them and a copy for her. And...she had kept her own records of her loan payoff. Surely those must be worth something?

She was strict on getting receipts from Mr. Thomas, and the banker had signed off on them! Including the final payment she'd made.

Glinda pulled herself to standing, relieved the throbbing in her head had abated enough. She carefully put her legs on the floor alongside her bed and stood. No sign of shakiness. Taking a deep breath, a little unsure of what might happen, she walked toward her bedroom door successfully.

Downstairs, she had a large box filled with records from the store. However, she also had used a small decorative box she'd gotten herself as a reward for all of her hard work. Only the size of her hand, it held a few bits and bobs, and the last receipt that Mr. Thomas had given her, proclaiming the loan was paid in full. She had kept it close by the counter so she could see it often, feel that surge of pride and comfort. How had she not thought of it sooner?

Of course, there was the problem in that there might not be a way to prove that it was Mr. Thomas's signature, but it was on bank stationary, so that added to her case.

Glinda made her way down the steps slowly. She was feeling much better but didn't dare rush and risk anything happening.

When she entered the store through the door between the stairs to the living quarters, Betty was just saying goodbye to a customer.

She whirled on her and scolded, "Just what are you doing out of bed?"

"I might have proof I paid off the loan," Glinda said. "The final receipt."

Betty's disapproving look melted away at once, replaced by an eager one. "Where is it?"

"That small decorative box I keep whatnots in," Glinda said, making her way to the counter.

"I know the one," Betty said, her eyes lighting up. "Oh! How wonderful you still have it!"

"Yes, I..." Glinda glanced around. "The box isn't here. Did you move it?"

"No." Betty shook her head. "I don't ever have cause to touch it."

Glinda refused to acknowledge the panic starting to rise as she touched the spot it had always been. "Where is it?" Glinda muttered, scanning the countertop.

"Maybe it fell to the shelf below," Betty said, stooping and beginning to rummage on the shelf where they kept the brown paper, twine, and some other items needed to run the store, but not necessarily use for customers.

"It must be here," Glinda said, turning to the shelves and counter behind her. "Where could it have gone?"

"We will find it," Betty said, her voice slightly muffled from where she was half under the counter.

"We must," Glinda whispered.

But an hour later, and then another hour, and another, every inch of her store, storeroom, and living quarters had been scoured and the small box that had sat for years, quite undisturbed next to her trusty notepad and pencil, was nowhere to be found.

Glinda finally accepted defeat, and dropped into a chair, her eyes still scanning around her, as though perhaps she'd missed the spot it was resting.

Betty poured them tea, heavily laced with sugar, and Glinda accepted hers wordlessly. What was there to say? To do?

The one thing that she thought she could do to save her store...and she'd mislaid it. Lost the only proof she had.

Though the tea was sweet, a bitter taste filled Glinda's mouth. As her eyes looked around the store once more, searching for a sign of the small box, she couldn't help but wonder how many more times she'd have the opportunity to see her beloved building before it was torn away.

Figuratively and literally.

Chapter 14

The quickest way to catch a no-gooder, Gus figured, was to tempt them with something. So, he needed to figure out just what that something was. He also needed to look like he wasn't in his right senses.

Time for a little acting. He'd watched his fair share of theatricals from the young folks at the school when they put on programs, and, of course, those gunslingers. He nearly laughed, remembering how they'd dressed up to put a stop to the troublemakers bothering the hotel owner.

Gus nodded. Right, then. He could do it too. He wandered through the town, making sure plenty of people saw him. First, as witnesses if he were to end up attacked. And to look harmless. Next, to see if he could figure out just who the person in red was. Any of them wearing a spot of the color, he made sure to talk loudly to tell them he was from out of town, had money to spend, and was there to have a good time.

After about an hour of meandering, Gus figured it was time. He began to whistle one of his favorite jigs. Maybe once he got back to Red Ridge with this statement from the banker, and Glinda's store was saved, she'd dance to it with him.

Time for the second act of his play. Gus stretched, being sure to take everything in as he did so, and wandered a little unsteady-like for good effect over toward the back of a row of buildings.

A large tree sat a way off, and he was sure the flash of red, whoever they might be, had to be behind it, as there wasn't really anywhere else to hide, and if he was being followed, that was the best spot for the person. He yawned loudly, settled himself on an empty crate, and reached into his shirt pocket.

Gus half pulled out his paper money, making sure it was wadded up to look like even more, then patted the pocket, as if he were making sure it was there.

Then he waited a moment and started to snore. Truth be told, he was getting right tuckered between the ride, the worry over Glinda, and all the walking, but Gus forced himself not to fall asleep for real.

Nothing happened, though.

Gus tried not to shift around restlessly or nod off, but playing possum was sure harder than he'd have thought.

He was tempted to reach up and pull his hat down over his eyes, then he could blink and not worry about holding his eyelids still. But if he did, then whoever was following him would know he wasn't really sleeping.

He realized he'd stopped snoring, and let out a snort, taking advantage of the moment to shift a little, since one leg was trying to fall asleep and had gotten all prickly. He hadn't realized just how hard this playacting was. It was right difficult for a body in more ways than one.

Bored now, and finding himself right drowsy, Gus started to count to keep himself focused, but it had the opposite effect, so he practiced sharpening his other senses while he waited. He sniffed at the air, and honed his ears, hoping he'd pick up something happening around him.

The softest of shuffles from a boot caught his attention, and he kept up his pretense. This was it. The person was nearby! At least, he hoped they were. This was getting mighty hard to keep doing.

The plan was to catch the feller's wrist when he reached out, do a little twist like Gavin had shown him, and then apply some pressure to a spot that Ryan Lundy had told him worked every time. Then Gus would tie him up, and ride like the wind for Red Ridge before he could be followed.

Gus waited. It sure was hard not to crack an eyelid open to see what was taking so long. He just needed the man to—

As fingers brushed against his chest, Gus let out a yell and grabbed at the hand. He hadn't planned to shout, it had just happened, but it might send people coming his way.

However, he hadn't counted on the other person moving so quickly, nor the words coming from them. "Hold up!"

Gus squinted, being on account the sun was so bright, not that he needed himself a pair of spectacles. Yet. Then he jolted. "Billy Madison! What are you doing trying to steal from an old man?"

"More like trying to push that money down so you don't get stole from," the gunslinger grumbled, dropping next to him on a barrel. He shook out his hand as he grimaced. "You just about caught me in that grip that I wouldn't have liked." Then he grinned. "Good job. It's a great move. Should have known you'd be expecting someone."

Gus chuckled. Then he took in the gunslinger and his red-checked shirt. "That you that's been following me?"

"It was."

"What are you doing here? Done told everyone I could handle this myself. Pretty sure I done said it more than once."

Billy pushed up his hat a little. "And I sure know you can. Didn't you almost give it to me just now? But you know Hannah. She was worried something fierce, and she came over to visit Mirabelle. Asked me to go too.

"Told her it wasn't a good idea, but then both those women ganged up on me! You know what that's like? It was safer out here, making sure I did what I was told. You know how much she loves you."

Gus grunted. "Still coulda said no."

"Coulda," Billy agreed. "Almost did. But then Meg started wailing about ya. Her eyes got so big and round... I was done for. You can't fault a man for that."

Gus fought back the lump in his throat at the scene Billy painted, even as he wanted to laugh at the mournful look on Billy's face. "Reckon I can't argue with that one, nor her ma. Still, I'd have handled myself just fine." He grinned. "Just needed to be sure whoever was following me was dealt with so I could ride back safe."

"That why you were sleeping?"

"Setting a trap," Gus corrected.

"Sure glad you saw it was me, and didn't spring it," Billy told him.

Gus grinned. "Knew what I was doing. Might be older but not in the pasture yet."

"You'll never be," Billy told him. "Any good news, though?" His eyes grew serious. Gus always appreciated how quick Billy could go from making jokes to all business. Made him right likable and pretty fearsome.

"Might be." Gus filled him in on his conversation with the banker.

When he was done, Billy let out a long whistle. "Phew. That guy sure was crooked. Wonder how many in Red Ridge he did that to."

"Makes me angry he might have done Glinda wrong, but I aim to get back quick as I can with this letter." Gus started toward the livery when he stopped. "Say, while you are here..."

"What do you need?" Billy asked.

"Jacob Cannon. You remember him?"

Billy scratched at his nose. "The circuit judge, right?"

"That's the one. Can you get word to him? Tell him to get over to Red Ridge, fast as he can?" Gus asked. "Don't rightly know where he might be right now."

"I don't either, but I know the towns he's judge in, and will send a message to each." Billy started walking away, and then requested his horse from the livery, paying the boy who rushed it out. Gus did the same with his mare, and mounted, heading back as fast as he could.

While what he had learned was good news, it wouldn't amount to a heap of beans if they couldn't get that official proof from the banker. He needed Gavin and the judge on the job right away.

The sun was setting as he started out, and Gus knew he wouldn't get back until dark. He rode hard, the night sky filling with stars above him. His attention caught on one twinkling mighty bright, like it was winking at him. A second later, it shot across the sky.

"Hope that's a good sign, not a bad one," he muttered. It sure was silly, but Gus made a wish, just in case it was that kind of star. Now, he just needed it to come true.

Chapter 15

It was nearly dawn, but Glinda hadn't slept at all. She was exhausted physically. But her mind wouldn't stop spinning, her fears and her worries taking on the face of Mr. Wimer and his lawyer, the taunting voices those of him.

Words he'd said kept playing in her mind. Dishonest. Trespassing illegally. Tear down the building.

As she sat on a wooden chair with a faded blue cushion on the seat, Glinda wrapped her warm knitted shawl around herself a little tighter and thought about Betty. She was being affected too, though she hadn't complained. The poor girl didn't deserve such a thing, not when none of this—including Glinda's inability to keep from losing such an important thing as her loan receipt—was her fault.

Right now, she felt like such a burden to those in the town. The sheriff was going out of his way to assist her, so was Betty's beau, Kent. Then, there was Gus. Her mind drifted toward him, and it was hard not to smile as she did. Gus had a way of doing that to her.

What was he doing right now? Had he made it back safely to Red Ridge? She desperately hoped so. Glinda wouldn't admit it to anyone, but while searching for the box, she'd been distracted. Not just from the pain in her head but also because of her worries over Gus.

Dixonburg wasn't terribly far, but it was still too far for her liking, especially when Gus was going there alone. She grappled with the fact that she was both concerned for his wellbeing, and selfishly wondering if he'd discovered anything that might help.

It was so hard to have faith in things working out, confidence that there would be a good resolution for both her and her store. Then, of course, there was also the fact that Gus had told her how he felt toward her. Had it happened too late? If she was forced to move, or to start fresh, would she even have the energy to rebuild her life, and also grow a romance?

It had been impulsive, her blowing him that kiss. Why, she'd acted without quite even realizing it. Maybe she should have done that sooner. Acted, not just thought.

With a sigh, Glinda rose and dressed for the day. Sitting and waiting for disaster only made it worse. Besides, maybe

Gus had made it back, and with some good news. Perhaps even with Mr. Thomas in tow!

As the sun's first rays cast a rose hue about her store, Glinda checked for the box again. It had to be somewhere. She wouldn't stop searching until she found it.

"Good morning, Aunt Glinda," Betty said, appearing with a tray in her hands. "I thought I'd find you here, so I brought you tea and toast for your breakfast."

"You are a dear," Glinda said. "But I don't know if I can eat. There's too much on my mind. I can't seem to do anything else but worry."

Sympathy filled her niece's eyes. "How is your head?" Betty asked.

"Better," Glinda said, speaking the truth. "It's my worry over the box that kept me awake."

"Shall I open early?" Betty asked. "I see Mrs. Blackstone coming this way. She looks quite impatient."

"How strange! The woman is usually anything but. It must be urgent. Yes, go ahead, and hopefully we can assist her in what she needs." Glinda retrieved her apron from the peg it hung on and tied the long strings around her waist. As the door opened, and the pastor's wife walked in, she smiled at her. "Good morning! How are you?"

"Ashamed," Mrs. Blackstone said, approaching with her basket, and an anxious expression on her face. "Do you remember when I came in here, and helped to load up my items into my basket?"

"I do," Glinda said, knitting her brows. She hoped that something wasn't wrong. Had she mistakenly shorted the pastor's wife? But if so, why would she be ashamed?

"I seem to have taken something on accident that wasn't mine," Mrs. Blackstone continued. "It has been eating me alive since I first saw."

"What do you mean?" Glinda asked.

"I hadn't fully put away the items in my basket that day, as Mirabelle came over feeling poorly," Mrs. Blackstone started.

"It's hard to be with child," Glinda clucked knowingly. "Though I only had the one, I can't imagine it's easier as time goes on."

"Nor I," the pastor's wife replied. "I was quite distracted, trying to ease her discomfort. I only just finished putting away my goods yesterday evening, and that's when I came across this." She reached into her basket, a moment later, pulling something out.

"My box!" Glinda gasped. "I've been searching everywhere!" She reached for the small wooden box, curling her fingers around it for a moment, grateful that it was safely in her possession again. "I thought I'd lost it," she said. "I am so grateful for its return."

"It's here?" Betty asked, rushing over.

"I do apologize, and didn't mean to cause you any distress," Mrs. Blackstone said, twisting her hands together. “I must have grabbed it by mistake. Please say you’ll forgive me.”

“Of course I will! No matter. Mistakes happen, goodness knows I’ve made my share, but I am so glad to have it returned.” Glinda raised the box’s lid, dipped her fingers into it, and pulled free the thing she’d been seeking.

The pastor’s wife continued talking, but Glinda scarcely heard her. She was too busy reading and rereading the signed letter from Mr. Thomas, stating that her loan for the land and the store had been paid in full.

Across the street, her eyes sought out the hotel. She had this proof now and would be sure to show the sheriff. And Mr. Wimer and his lawyer. But would this be enough to save her store? There was only one way to find out. She’d need to show the sheriff first, so she had him as a witness if something were to happen to the letter.

“Betty, can you watch the store?” Glinda burst out, hoping that she hadn’t interrupted anything important being said. “I’ve got to see the sheriff urgently, and show him this receipt.”

Her niece answered, but Glinda hardly registered it, instead rushing through the shop door, her eyes locked on two men who were walking down the street.

Chapter 16

"You did good," Gavin said, setting the letter Gus had brought him down on his kitchen table. "I will write Mr. McGuire right away for specifics."

"Just wish I'd have been allowed to bring something more helpful back, but I understand," Gus said. "Not none of my business who done paid what and when in that town."

Winnie set a plate before him with a stack of flapjacks, and he reached for the molasses as she set another stack in front of Gavin.

"I have plenty," she said. "Eat up."

"Sure will," Gus told her happily, spearing up his first bite. "Never met a flapjack I didn't like."

"I assume you've not had a chance to get over to Mrs. Stover yet?" Gavin asked.

He shook his head. "No, didn't want to disturb her in the middle of the night or alarm her. Also wanted to be sure you got this right away, in case something happened to it. Then you done seen it too."

"And you say Billy is sending word to Judge Cannon?" Gavin asked.

Gus mumbled around a mouthful of breakfast, "Yep."

"Then soon as you're done, let's head to town. I'll message the banker in Dixonburg, and we ought to check in on Mrs. Stover. This might at least alleviate a few of her worries." The sheriff hesitated and added, almost gently, "She collapsed yesterday."

The fork fell from Gus's hand, and his heart near burst from his chest. The last of the flapjack seemed to stick in his throat, but he was on his feet, heading toward the door, when Gavin stopped him.

"She's okay now. It was stress, Doc said. Made her stay in bed. I thought you should know, because I'm not sure she'd tell anyone willingly."

"I understand," Gus said. "She's a woman who's been on her own for so long, she ain't used to letting things slow her down." He coughed, the tightness easing in his chest, but the flapjack still stuck there with the molasses. Not fear. Not him. Nothing made him scared.

Except for the idea of losing Glinda.

Gus swallowed and coughed again.

"Here," Winnie said, pressing his mug into his hand. "Drink this before you go. Don't want to be sputtering all over her. She might not take kindly to it."

Gus drained the mug, grateful. "Thank you, Winnie. For breakfast too. You tell those siblings of yours I said hello."

"I will," she promised, then kissed Gavin's cheek as he dropped his hat on his head and went outside.

Gavin mounted quickly, his horse already waiting for him. Nick, Winnie's younger brother, had taken to doing things before they needed doing. A fine trait for a young man who wanted to be just like his brother-in-law. Gus wondered if one day he might even be the sheriff.

They rode toward town, the horses kicking up dust, passing by cattle and waving wheat in the fields, and a handful of folks pulling wagons in or out of town.

When they pulled up to the livery, Gus dropped down, and took off for Glinda's store, not looking to see if the sheriff was with him. He was sure the man was.

They fell into step together just as the general store's door opened, and Glinda came rushing out. "I'm so glad to see you!" she called, waving a paper in her hands.

Witnesses be darned, Gus didn't care. He rushed over to her, fast as his creaky knees would let him, and grabbed hold of her. "What's this about you falling over?"

Her cheeks pinked, and she smacked at him. "Pish. It's nothing. Just the worry, is all. Got a mite dizzy and..."

"And what?" Gus asked, squinting as he looked her over. Maybe he oughter see about a pair of spectacles. If he was going to take a chance and ask to be courting Glinda, he didn't want to miss anything about her.

"Struck my head," she said softly, not meeting his eyes even as her hand went to the spot hidden by her hair.

Gus sucked in his breath, catching himself just before he wheezed. "Well then, guess I'm working at the store today. I'll get word to Hannah."

"But—"

"Not letting you out of my sight, woman," Gus growled. "Got to take care of you."

Her face was bright red now, but she didn't protest. Gus sure hoped that meant she'd be delighted to have his company, and not that she was about to whack him with one of her cast-iron frying pans.

"What's that you have?" Gavin asked her.

Glinda's face lit up. "My receipt! The final loan payment, on bank stationary, and signed and dated by Mr. Thomas himself!"

"That's great news," Gavin said, taking it from her. He held out an envelope. "Gus got this for you as well."

Glinda glanced at him, and Gus grinned, hooking his thumbs at his belt. "That's right. That's a little more good news." His face fell slightly, as he added, "At least, I hope it's not bad news."

He watched as she read through the letter from the Dixonburg banker, and then breathed a sigh of relief.

"Can I assume, Sheriff, that you are going to request this information?" she asked.

Gavin nodded. "I'm about to send a letter, and have it delivered by Winnie's brother. He's meeting me here in an hour. Billy Madison has already gotten word to Judge Cannon, and he's going to be making his way over here as soon as possible, I suspect. We should hear from him soon."

"Oh, thank goodness. I don't know what I'd do without you wonderful gentlemen," Glinda said, though her eyes were fixed on Gus.

He straightened up a little, and offered, "Can't say for sure, but reckon we might be saying farewell to that Mr. Wimer and his lawyer soon."

"Now, we can't be too hasty in saying that," Gavin warned. "We've not seen his evidence. Could be his is irrefutable."

Glinda's face fell. "You are right. I was putting my cart before the horse."

"But there's also no need to be distressed," Gavin said. "Just...cautiously optimistic. While I don't get the final say, the judge does, I can say it's looking good for you."

"Meaning, we get to send that man on his way," Gus said, slapping his knee. "Good riddance!"

"Wouldn't that be wonderful," she said. "I—" A frown came over her face as she broke off whatever thought had come over her.

Gus and Gavin followed her eyes, where a wagon was coming into town, much faster than it ought to. Townsfolk were scrambling to get out of the way.

The sheriff started toward the wagon, gun already in hand. Shots were fired from the wagon, and screams filled the air.

Gus pushed Glinda behind him, shouting, "Git in the store!" and ran toward Gavin.

He'd worked too hard to try and help Glinda to let anything happen to her now.

There was another shot, and the horses on the wagon screamed, the sound more terrifying than anything he'd heard for a while. Out of nowhere, Billy appeared and ran alongside the wagon, jumping up to grab onto the harnesses, doing that sweet talk he had a way of doing with horses as he swung onto one's back.

Somehow, Billy was able to slow the wagon, but a man was bent over in the seat. Billy kept his attention on the horses, soothing them as he climbed down and held them firmly.

Gavin roared, "Someone get the doctor!"

"I'm already here," Aiden called, running over with Nora at his side.

Gus helped to pull the man from the front of the wagon, a crimson stain blooming over his shirt.

"What happened?" Dr. Rycroft asked.

The man groaned. "Horses got spooked by something. Was cleaning my gun on the ride, and it went off when I tried to set it down and grab the reins."

"Luckily, the second shot didn't hit someone in town," Gavin said sternly. "You should have known better."

"Nora, I need—" Aiden began.

"Already have it," Billy's sister answered, handing over a neatly folded bundle of cloth.

Gus stepped back, letting the man and his horses be attended to. He glanced toward Glinda's store, where he could see her watching anxiously. He waved her over, and she hurried across the street.

"Just an accident," Gus told her.

"That's right. Today won't be the day we need our guns," Gavin said. "I appreciate days like that."

Billy came up to them. "Got word to Judge Cannon. Got a reply too. He's on his way." His grin fell. "But no promises, Mrs. Stover."

"I understand," Glinda said quietly. "Do you...do you think I ought to let Mr. Wimer and his lawyer know so they can have all of their papers ready when the judge gets here? I don't want to waste his time. And, truthfully, I want this to be over as quickly as possible."

"That's a good idea," Gus said.

"I'll join you," Gavin said. "You don't need to be going there without a representative of the law."

"I agree," Billy said. "I'll finish up here, if you want."

Gavin nodded his thanks. "Give me just a moment. I'll be right along."

"We can wait over here," Glinda said, pointing to a bench near the hotel.

Gus followed her, and when she took her seat, he sat next to her. His heart was thudding something fierce still. He wasn't sure, though, if it was because they were so close or because of the excitement they'd just had. The old ticker had been wound up something fierce the last few days.

"Gus," Glinda said quietly, "I want to tell you something."

"What's that?" he asked, his pulse speeding up again. He always worried when someone used that phrase.

"I've never had anyone put themselves between me and the danger before," she told him. "I'm grateful to you. And for your offer to help in my store today. But I don't want you thinking that I'm some weak woman who can't take care of herself."

"Aw, shucks, Glinda!" Gus said, turning to see her better. "I don't think that."

"What do you think, then?" she asked, hands clasped in her lap and her eyes fixed on them.

Gus thought for a moment. How could he say it where it made sense? He wasn't the best at talking. Not to women.

He sat there so long that Glinda started to stand. "Wait!" Gus said. "I'm just formulating my words. I ain't used to such conversations."

She stilled and looked at him expectantly.

Gus pushed out his lips, then said, "Don't know how long it's been—well, that's a lie. I do. Was the first time I saw you. But I've always felt something here for you." He pressed into his heart. "And the thought of losing you somehow, in any way, well, it does something to me. Can't rightly explain it, but I don't want you not to be here."

"In Red Ridge?" she asked softly.

"In Red Ridge, on this bench, with me," Gus said. "Any of it. I—"

Gavin walked up just then. "Thanks for waiting."

"Of course," Glinda said, rising.

Gus tried not to let his shoulders slump in disappointment. He felt the softest of brushes on his arm and glanced down, wide-eyed, to see Glinda resting her fingers there, looking at him hesitantly.

Squaring his shoulders, Gus patted her hand, and they went into the hotel. Polished wood and colorful rugs met his eye. As did Kent Jackson, Betty's beau, rushing over.

"I didn't expect to see you," Kent said. "Has something happened?" He looked at the sheriff.

"We were hoping to speak with Mr. Wimer and his lawyer," Glinda said, her voice quivering slightly.

"I'm so sorry," Kent said. "They both left this morning. I don't know where they went, and I don't know when they'll be back."

Chapter 17

Glinda's mother used to claim that a watched pot never boiled. That was wrong, actually. If one watched the liquid inside long enough, eventually tiny bubbles that clung to the sides of the vessel would break free and then turn into a rapid rising of larger bubbles.

Much like the ones in her stomach.

However, unlike the pot that would eventually do its intended purpose with long enough of a wait, life was unpredictable, and Glinda was quite tired of waiting for something to happen.

Three days had passed since Gus had given the news that the banker in Dixonburg was willing to share the information he had with Sheriff Jefferson and Judge Cannon. However, also in those three days, Glinda hadn't seen Mr. Wimer or his lawyer.

The hotel had confirmed that neither man had checked out, but they'd also said no one had seen them. Glinda wasn't sure what to make of that. It made her nervous. Were the two of them up to something? Gathering more evidence to support their case? She wished she knew.

"Got them sacks of beans stacked," Gus said, walking out from the storeroom. "You need me for anything else before I get me a sit down?"

"Not a thing," Glinda said, marveling at how the tension that had been a near constant companion to her eased at the sight of him.

The last few days, Gus had stayed by her side, leaving only to go home at night and return the next morning. At first, Glinda had been a little worried. She was used to being on her own, running things her way, and doing what needed to be done. She hadn't been sure how it would be, having Gus there underfoot and wanting to nose his way into how she did things.

So, it came as a great surprise that he was quite content to let her direct him, and he'd settle down with a mug and a bite between those moments, or one of the newspapers he special ordered each week.

As he eased into a chair near the stove, picking up one of the newspapers, she said, "Thank you again. I appreciate your help."

He grinned at her. "Remember now, you just boss me around. This here is your place. If I get underfoot, you tell me. I'll sit right still for a time with a slice of pie and a newspaper or a game of checkers with one of the boys."

She laughed at that. "I appreciate that as well."

He just winked at her and picked up the newspaper, already shaking his head over one of the articles. Glinda went back to the task she'd been doing—looking out the large glass window where she could see the hotel, and fretting.

"You got the law and the proof on your side," Gus said, not even looking up when she glanced over.

"I know I do, but sometimes, that doesn't matter," Glinda said thoughtfully. "There are instances where justice isn't served, and the innocent are wrongly punished."

"The world sure ain't perfect," Gus agreed. His eyes wandered outside the store and to those passing by as well. "Reckon that's where we got to work on building up our patience and our faith."

"You're a good man," Glinda murmured, and picked up the broom. How calm he was. The complete opposite of her. If she couldn't keep herself from worrying, she might as well find something to do while worrying.

She swept the store, carefully collecting the dirt a customer had tracked in on his boots. Several women came in, and Glinda had the temporary distraction of waiting on them.

"Aunt Glinda, the delivery is here," Betty called from the back, where she'd been taking inventory of the storeroom.

"You just direct me, and I'll do the lifting," Gus said, standing.

"I have to admit," Glinda said, as they walked toward the door that led to where the delivery wagon was, "I am getting used to you being around. I'm not sure how I'll manage once things go back to normal. That is, if they do."

"Aw, shucks, Glinda. I told you I'd do anything for you. This ain't nothing."

The wagon driver started pointing to crates before Glinda could say anything more, and Gus and Betty unloaded the supplies, carrying them into the storeroom, while she signed for the delivery.

"Aunt Glinda," Betty said, standing next to her as the final crate was unloaded, "Kent has offered us a place at the hotel. Just...just in case."

"I hope it doesn't come to that," Glinda said, "but do tell him I appreciate it."

"I will," Betty said. "Are you still fine if I leave to have lunch with him?"

"Of course! Go right ahead," Glinda said, locking the back door. They walked into the store and she added, "I've got Gus here if I need anything."

"Sure do," Gus said, from his spot by the stove.

Betty hurried away, and Glinda took advantage of the moment without customers to check on the meal she had going upstairs. She returned with two bowls of the creamy vegetable stew and handed one to Gus.

"You spoil me," he said.

"Consider it payment," she answered. Then, though she didn't know why she said it, Glinda added, "You're a right fine man, Gus. It's a wonder you've not been snatched up before now."

"I could say the same about you," he told her, blowing on a spoonful of stew. "If I'm not being too forward, why didn't you ever remarry?"

Glinda set down her bowl to pick up her teacup. "At first, it was because I wasn't sure I wanted to. I had my boy to look after, and the store."

"And later?" Gus asked.

Her cheeks colored and her eyes fell to the amber liquid. "Later, there was someone I was interested in. But I wasn't sure he cared about me." They sat in silence for a moment before she ventured, "But why didn't you ever marry?"

"Almost did," he told her. "Got there to the church and everything."

Glinda's eyes widened. She hadn't known that. "What happened? That must have been before I moved here."

"It were about..." Gus pushed his lips out in thought, "two or three months afore you got here. Yep, thought I was going to marry Megan Hisemith. Thought she thought it too. Turned out she had fallen in love with a cowboy. They were pitching woo behind my back." He swallowed hard.

"I'm so sorry," Glinda said, reaching out to rest her hand on his arm. "That must have been so terrible to discover."

"Was worse, waiting 'round at the church, getting them sympathetic looks." Gus was quiet. "Took a while before I got over it."

"And..." Glinda took a deep breath, "and no one caught your eye later?"

"One did," Gus said. His voice grew quiet. "Beautiful smile, kind and capable, strong and not one to mince words. Just the sort of woman I wanted. Gave me her hankie once. Still have it."

It was foolish, she knew, but Glinda fought down the jealousy that consumed her. She had no right to feel envy over a woman from his past, nor the fact that Gus obviously hadn't gotten over whatever woman this was he was talking about.

"Why did you not...pursue?" she managed to ask.

His eyes met hers. "Well, she was right busy raising that baby of hers and running a store," he told her, his voice low. "And I reckon I was right scared she didn't want me butting in. By the time I done worked up the courage to tell her I liked her, somehow, a lot of years had passed, and here we are. Sitting over a bowl of stew. Mighty fine stew, I might add."

"Do you mean," Glinda whispered. "It was..."

"It was always you," Gus told her, putting a stop to the thoughts that had been swarming her imagination. "I just didn't know how to tell you. I'm sorry for that. I've wasted a lot of time, and now, instead of being the kind of man you need or might want, I'm old. Ain't spry no more."

"Who needs spry, when you have a man who can always tell you the weather?" Glinda asked with a small smile. "Or can converse about any subject because he's so well-read?"

Gus sat a little taller. "That's all true," he agreed. "I'm a feller of many talents."

"I'm older too," Glinda said quietly, almost in a sigh.

"Aged, like a fine cheese," Gus corrected her. "None of that green stuff that might make your belly revolt it's so wild."

She had to laugh then. At least he hadn't compared her to a mule, like he might have. But as she opened her mouth to ask if he really still had that hankie she'd given him years and years before, Betty came rushing through the shop's door, breathless.

"What's wrong?" Glinda asked, already starting toward her.

"The judge is riding into town," Betty said, panting slightly. "And with him is Mr. Wimer and his lawyer."

Chapter 18

Judge Jacob Cannon sat at the schoolteacher's desk, the place he always decided his cases when he came to town, scratching some notes down with a pencil onto a sheet of paper. Gus glanced to his left at Glinda, who was sitting there, hands in her lap, every bit of her as tense as could be.

"The cases heard today," Judge Cannon said suddenly, looking up at the assembled room, "will be that of Morris versus Donvan, Stover versus Wimer, and Smith versus Clyde."

"Second," Glinda murmured. "Thank goodness. I don't know how much longer I can wait. The stress is..." She took a deep breath and blew it out slowly.

Judge Cannon began talking to the first group of men, letting them share their sides of the story. So far, things were calm, but Gus knew it wouldn't stay that way for long. Morris was a firecracker with a fuse lit. Anyone would say so as witness.

If needed, Gus planned to be one of Glinda's witnesses. While he couldn't vouch for having seen her make her loan payments, he sure planned to let the judge know she was nothing if not an honest and hardworking woman.

Gavin had gotten the information from the Dixonburg banker, and held that, and Glinda's final loan payment receipt, in his care. There wasn't much more they could do. He was just grateful they were getting a hearing, and that their town had a sheriff—one who was honest and couldn't be bought off.

His eyes narrowed as he imagined what might happen if Carson still ran the town. Glinda's store might have been gone already, and Carson's pocket a little heavier.

When the judge had ridden in the day before, Wimer and his lawyer with him, there had been a few moments of worry that the men all knew each other, or that Wimer had somehow laid out his side already.

Thankfully, that hadn't been the case. They'd simply been sharing a stagecoach.

"I see no wrongdoings here," Judge Cannon said, startling Gus from his meandering thoughts. "Merely two men who ought to work together to ensure that their fences are in good repair. When your land touches another, you've the choice of each building a fence, with a small gap between, building a fence and sharing the responsibility for the costs and care of it, or simply taking your chances. I suggest the second method."

The men who stood before him muttered something and nodded, stepping back.

"Now, Stover and Wimer," the judge said. He rested his hands on the desk. "Please approach and tell me your situation."

Glinda stood, trembling just a little as she walked toward the front of the room. Her face was looking a little green, and Gus watched in concern. Gavin stood nearby. He had to be neutral, what with being the law and all, but that morning, he'd promised he was on her side entirely.

Wimer and his lawyer approached as well. "Your Honor, if I may go first?" he asked.

The judge nodded.

"I am Charles Wimer. This is my family's lawyer, Duncan White. I came to Red Ridge a little over a week ago to see the land that my father had acquired when a loan defaulted and he took over the payments. You can imagine my surprise when I saw Mrs. Stover not only running a business but also living there. The land is mine, and I intend to build there. Mrs. Stover is in violation of the law and needs to leave."

"Do you have evidence of this loan?" the judge asked.

"I do," the lawyer said, handing over a few sheets of paper.

Judge Cannon looked at each carefully. "Have you anything more to add before Mrs. Stover speaks?"

"No, sir," Wimer said.

"Mrs. Stover?" the judge said. "It is your turn to speak in your defense."

"Yes, sir," Glinda said, twisting her hands together. "When we came to Red Ridge, my husband and I, he took out a loan. When he died a short time later, I was determined to pay it off, and that's just what I did. I made my payments each month to the banker, Mr. Thomas. He wrote it down in his ledger and also gave me receipts.

"Every bit of that loan was paid off. Until Mr. Wimer came to town, I had no idea that someone else thought they owned my land."

"And have you any proof of this?" Judge Cannon asked.

"Some," Gavin said, stepping forward. "Mrs. Stover entrusted me with these documents. This one here is the receipt from the bank saying the loan was paid in full. The banker who replaced Mr. Thomas can attest that this is the bank's letterhead and that the signature matches that of Mr. Thomas."

"I can," Mr. Logan said, standing.

"What else do you have?" Judge Cannon asked, after he nodded at the banker.

"I have here a letter from the banker in Dixonburg, who took over for Mr. Thomas. Mr. Thomas was accused of fraud, and in situations very similar to that of Mrs. Stover." Gavin offered the letters from the Dixonburg banker.

Judge Cannon read through the papers slowly. The room was so quiet, Gus could hear himself blink. He wondered if he should approach the judge, speak up for Glinda.

The judge set the letters down and asked, "I have all of the evidence before me of each of your claims to this land?"

Glinda and Wimer nodded.

Judge Cannon frowned and studied the documents before him again. "This is a difficult situation, indeed. Each of you has proof that the land is yours. In fact, everything looks to be in order with what you've given me, Mr. Wimer."

The man stood a little straighter.

"Yet, Mrs. Stover, you not only have evidence you've paid your loan, but that the man who you made payments to was dishonest." Judge Cannon tapped his fingers in thought.

"This is neither the first time I've heard such a story, nor the first time I've heard of Mr. Thomas. Several years ago, I actually was the judge who was given the evidence that Mr. Thomas, the banker who took your payments, and those of many others, was keeping them. Not only that, it was proven that he was offering the loans to others.

"You see, he had a clever little scheme," Judge Cannon said, addressing the crowd. "If he took payments for one loan, but acted as though the person weren't making payments, he could resell that loan and pocket the cash from the person who'd taken it over. I'm afraid that appears to be what's happened in this case. The bank got its money, and no one was the wiser that he was filling his pockets."

"Then who is the rightful owner of the land?" Wimer's lawyer asked. "We have proof of our payments!"

"You do," Judge Cannon said. "However, your loan information is dated after Mrs. Stover's."

"Because we took over the loan payments!" Wimer said.

Gus started to stand, just as the sheriff stepped toward Wimer. "Don't interrupt the judge," Gavin warned, his arms crossed over his chest.

Wimer nodded, and Gus hesitated, half sitting, half standing. Didn't seem he was needed. Was that a good thing? Or bad?

Judge Cannon addressed Wimer. "Yes, but those payments began after the date that her loan was paid in full. There is enough evidence to prove that her documents are legitimate, and that the land and everything on it belongs to Glinda Stover in full. We may never know if it was her money or yours that paid for her loan or ended up in his pocket."

"But my family paid for the loan!" Wimer protested. "We—"

"Were unfortunately victims of a con man," Judge Cannon said. "I'm sorry for that. You were paying on something that didn't belong to the bank, and didn't belong to Mr. Thomas.

"Restitution is owed to you, but with Mr. Thomas dead, you may not get it. You are welcome to pursue locating his family and trying to recover your money, but the land here in Red Ridge belongs to Mrs. Stover. This matter has been decided."

Wimer stood there, his mouth working open and closed. His lawyer patted him on the shoulder and started to leave the schoolhouse. Wimer followed him, leaning close to the man, whispering.

Gus stood and made his way over to Glinda. "Your store is safe!" he told her. "I was about to go up and ask to speak, but I weren't needed at all. Fine judge, he is."

"Yes, and I'm so grateful," she said. "I also appreciate your help in all of this. But...why do I feel so badly for Mr. Wimer?"

"It's because you're a good person," Gus told her.

"I...I want to tell him no hard feelings," Glinda said, starting toward the door.

"You reckon that's wise? Man might not be too happy," Gus said, catching up to her.

"You'll be with me, so I'm not the least bit worried," Glinda said, sliding her arm through his.

Gus stood a little taller and led her outside. Was she meaning that? He thought so, but with a woman like Glinda, independent, confident, was she just saying that because he was her friend? Gus wasn't sure he'd ever felt so confused.

Wimer and his lawyer were walking toward the hotel but stopped when Glinda called out to them.

"Mrs. Stover," Mr. Wimer said, his voice tight as he turned. "Here to gloat?"

"Not at all," Glinda said. "I'm here to tell you that I'm sorry you were taken advantage of. I won't lie, I'm grateful to still have my store. I'm older, and the idea of starting over again was terrifying. The thought of all I'd worked to build being destroyed might have made me speak in ways that I wouldn't ordinarily. I hope you'll forgive me, if I said anything that might have hurt your feelings."

The man looked at her in surprise. Gus wasn't shocked, though. He always knew Glinda was right classy.

"Thank you," he finally said, then shrugged. "It's a loss, to be sure, but it wasn't devastating. My family has plenty of money, and this won't even be missed. The resort was simply going to be something I did to get us more. The amount of the loan is inconsequential. It's the fact that we were taken advantage of, that's what I dislike."

Gus grunted. "Nobody likes that. But that much money? Reckon that's not a problem I'll ever have, but I hope you do something good with it, young feller, not just make more and more."

"I do," Wimer said. "There's an orphan school over in Hackberry Falls, Kansas, that I support, among other things. I wish you both the best in your future endeavors. Now, if you'll excuse me, I must pack. I will be departing shortly." Wimer nodded at them and walked inside the hotel.

"I'm glad it's over," Glinda sighed. "Perhaps tonight I'll be able to sleep."

Gus nodded. He wanted to ask her to dinner to celebrate. Wanted to ask her for a stroll under the moon he was sure would be shining all pretty. Wanted to tell her how he felt again.

But for some reason, the words wouldn't come up. Now that the possibility of her losing her store and having to leave town had passed, his throat was as dry as the dust on his boots. All the doubts he'd been feeling swirled around in him.

When he'd told her inside her store how it was her he'd always loved, her he'd always wanted, she hadn't given him an answer. Of course, Betty had come bursting in, but they'd had a few opportunities afterward, and she hadn't said a thing.

So, neither did he.

Gus swallowed, trying to make his throat work. Could only mean one thing that she hadn't answered. She didn't feel for him the way he felt for her. All the signs seemed to be pointing to that.

Then there was the matter her store had been saved. That meant she didn't need him anymore. There was no reason to stop by so often, to be there to protect her when there was nothing she needed protecting from. Gus was sure he hadn't felt so useless in a long time. Not since that fever had come through, and he was going around visiting folks with nothing more than peppermint or chamomile tea, pretending it was a cure-all.

"Gus, would you—"

"Sorry, Glinda," Gus managed. "I—I gotta hurry back to the ranch."

"But—"

He didn't wait to see what she said, just left in a hurry, like the coward he was because he couldn't stand to hear her answer if it was a no, if he asked her all his questions.

Like he'd just told Wimer, nobody liked to be made a fool of.

Chapter 19

The bell over the shop door let out its soft jingle, and Glinda looked eagerly toward it. Then, just as quickly, her face fell. The one person she'd been hoping to see—longing to see—wasn't there, standing in the doorway, ambling over to her, a grin on his face.

"I won't take it personally that you are looking at me like that," Hannah said with a sweet laugh as she approached.

"No, please don't," Glinda hastened to assure her. "I'm sorry. I was just expecting...well, I was hoping to see someone, that's all."

"Would that someone be our local weather teller?" Hannah asked.

"It would be," Glinda said with a sigh. "I've not seen him since the judge was here and heard my case."

"He's not left the ranch," Hannah said quietly.

"Is he ill?" Glinda asked, immediately worrying. "He left so abruptly. It wasn't at all like him."

Hannah was quiet for a moment, and placed her shopping basket down on the counter. "In a way," she admitted. "It's not my place to say, but I suspect it's a broken heart."

That wasn't at all what Glinda had thought she'd say. In fact, the moment she had said 'I suspect,' Glinda's heart had nearly stopped. She had reached for the counter to steady herself, hoping that she wouldn't faint again.

"Do you..." Glinda sucked in a deep breath. "Do you think he'd..."

"I think he'd love to see you," Hannah told her. "To know you were thinking of him. I have the wagon. You can ride back with me, and someone can return you to town when you are ready."

Glinda hesitated. She wanted to go, could easily close the store. But...should she? Would he welcome seeing her? The last time she'd tried to talk to him, Gus had left abruptly.

"Is Betty here to mind the store?" Hannah asked.

"Yes, she's upstairs checking on the stew. It's just ... I worry about if he would want to see me."

"Well," Hannah said slowly, "while I don't know what's going on between the two of you, I do know that nothing makes Gus happier than seeing you."

Glinda tried not to grimace. "I hope he will be. I tried to talk to him after the judge sided in my favor, and he ran away."

"Sometimes people do that when they get scared," Hannah said.

"He didn't even wait to see what I was trying to say!" Glinda said. "There was nothing to be scared of!"

Hannah laughed. "Men are a strange lot, at times. That's why I feel so fortunate to have Eli."

"He's a good man," Glinda agreed. "His friends are too."

The door between her living quarters and the store creaked open, and Betty appeared. "Hello, Hannah."

"How are you? And Kent?" Hannah asked.

"Feeling much better now that we don't have to worry about Aunt Glinda's store," Betty said.

"I think I'm going to ride with Hannah to her ranch and check on Gus," Glinda told her niece. "Hannah said he's...he's been poorly."

"Oh no!" Betty said, worry filling her face. "Yes, go ahead. I'll mind the store."

"Give me just a moment," Glinda said. "Betty can fill your order while I get ready."

She hurried away to hang up her apron, get her second-best hat—the one with small sprigs of greenery—and check her reflection in the small mirror in her room, trying unsuccessfully to pin back that one piece of hair that always slid out.

"Oh well, that'll just have to do," Glinda said. "After all, if I dress up too much, folks'll whisper."

She went down the stairs, walking into the store just as Betty said, "Anything else for you?"

"That is all," Hannah said. "Eli will come for our winter supplies with the wagon once it's in. Gus says it's going to be a harsh one, and I believe him."

"I've heard that," Glinda said. "I agree with him. We are overdue for one."

"Oh dear," Betty said. "I don't like the sound of that. The two of you have given me goosebumps!"

"We'll all be fine," Hannah assured her. "It just means being stuck at home, and having a little extra on hand is important." She turned to Glinda. "Are you ready?"

"I am."

The door swung open just then and Kent wandered in. "Ladies."

"See you soon," Glinda said, leaving and feeling a little better that Betty wouldn't be entirely alone. It felt as though she'd asked Betty to mind the store on her own far too often. On the one hand, the place would be hers one day, and Betty was far more than capable, but she didn't want her niece to feel overworked.

That was a feeling she knew all too well, and sometimes looked back at those early days when she'd been running the store and bringing up her son, and wondered how she'd managed to do it all.

Though there was small talk, Glinda's mind kept returning to why she was there. Was it a foolish thing to do, going to see Gus? Why, he might no longer be interested in her. It wasn't like she had much to offer, especially at her age.

"Here we are," Hannah said, climbing into the wagon.

Glinda followed her, and soon they were bumping and swaying over the dirt road out to Hannah's ranch.

She'd never been out this way, and Glinda glanced all around, taking in the homes she'd not seen before. "I feel nervous," she suddenly said. "As though I won't be welcome."

"Nonsense," Hannah told her. "You are welcome. I've invited you. If you choose to spend your time talking with Gus or if you decide to come back to the kitchen for some tea and a cookie—mine, not Meg's—then that's your choice."

"Thank you," Glinda murmured.

It wasn't too long at all before they arrived, the house and the outbuildings rising before them. Glinda squinted against the sun, holding one hand up to block it slightly, as she sought Gus.

There were ranch hands moving around here and there, but she didn't spot the familiar, slightly stooped figure of Gus.

"The bunkhouse is right there," Hannah said, pointing. "It's where he sleeps, and often is when he's not working outside or playing with the children."

"Then that is where I'll look first," Glinda said. "Thank you."

She climbed down from the wagon and headed toward the building Hannah had indicated. Before the door, she hesitated. Did one just walk inside? Knock first? She really wasn't sure, but considering it was the bunkhouse, where men lived, she thought she'd best knock, in case one of them was in the middle of changing his clothes.

Before she could lose her nerve, Glinda knocked briskly.

A long moment passed, and just as she'd raised her closed hand to do it again, the door opened wide, and Gus stared at her, jaw dropping.

"Hello," Glinda said.

A small word, not good enough, but she hoped it would convey what she was thinking. How she was feeling. That she missed him, was worried about him.

"Woman, not sure it's proper for you to be here." Gus squinted at her, that familiar look he often gave when he was thinking.

"That's why I'm outside, instead of in," she told him.

"True, true," he answered.

There was silence between them for a long time—before they both spoke at the same time.

"Why are you—"

"I was worr—"

They stopped, neither speaking. Finally, Glinda said, "I was worried about you."

"Jest right busy," Gus told her, not meeting her eyes as he looked down.

"I've...I've missed you," Glinda said, pressing forward. "I have also been afraid that I did something to upset you, and that's why you left so suddenly."

He met her eyes then, and shook his head. "Shucks. You couldn't ever do that. Least, I don't think you could. No, that weren't it."

"What was it then?" Glinda asked.

"Was feeling a little like I weren't needed," Gus told her, shrugging slightly.

"Not needed? Oh Gus! I need you more than anything," Glinda told him, her voice wobbling slightly. "I kept thinking about what you'd said, about the woman you'd wanted...me...all those years ago. It's made me realize something."

"That so?" Gus asked.

"Yes. What if I don't have but a few more years to give you? Is that fair? Is that why you left so suddenly? You realized it too? Changed your mind about liking me? Am I too late? For a chance to have your love for my own?"

Chapter 20

Gus cleared his throat, and tried not to look like he was as nervous as he felt. Here she'd done gone and asked the question and his mind had hung out the gone fishin' sign. It was as blank as Meg's slate when she was supposed to copy down her spelling words the other night before dinner.

Something managed to work its way through his mind, and he spit it out, not even thinking about what the words were. "Things...things going good at the store?" he asked.

That wasn't what he meant to say, but it was what had come out, so Gus hooked his thumbs into his waistband and acted as though that's what he'd meant.

She blinked several times, but nodded. "For the most part. There's the small problem, though, of you not being there. I'd gotten so used to it. Now, I am not quite sure how I'm going to manage." Her eyes near bored through him, just like that worm he'd watched eating at a fallen leaf earlier.

"You just let me know when you need something done," Gus told her. "I'll be right there."

"It's more than that," Glinda told him. "It's about what I just said. And I...I'd like an answer, Gus."

He nodded, then stepped a little closer. "How about we go on a little walk?" he told her. "There's a creek not far away. Better scenery, and then we don't have folks listening in. These fellers can tease a man relentlessly."

"I understand," Glinda answered, stepping back a little to let him out the door.

Once he was fully outside, Gus led the way, Glinda walking alongside him. It didn't take too long to go from the bunkhouse to the garden, and then a short distance away.

He paused, as he always did, at the spot where Hannah had near fought for her life against her evil brother-in-law, and said a quick thanks that things had turned out the way they had, and then walked a few dozen steps away, to a favorite spot of his, a log covered in soft green moss, but still sturdy enough to sit on.

"Sit a spell?" he asked.

"Thank you," Glinda answered, and arranged herself, smoothing her skirt down.

Gus sat next to her, just a little space between them, and wondered just how he could say what it was he was thinking. Was there a better way than to just blurt it out? Something smooth like, something that was romantic or exciting or just right?

He rubbed at his jaw, and said, "Fact is, I've been loving you for so long, I'd do anything for the chance to do that for reals, not just in my mind. You ain't too late for me, Glinda. Reckon I wondered a time or two if I'm too young for you, on account of my birthday being almost a year after yours."

Her lips quirked up, and a hint of laughter was on her face as she said, "That must be why you are so strong and have so much more energy to do all you do."

"Could be," he admitted with a shrug. "Though, these old bones are slowing down a mite."

"If you really have felt that way about me," Glinda said softly, looking down into her lap, "then why did you leave so suddenly the other day? I was so worried about you."

Gus pushed his lips out. "Well, now, that's a little embarrassing."

"I promise never to say anything or tease you about it," she reassured him. "I just was fearful that I had done something."

"You couldn't never do nothing. I reckon I was feeling a little down. Here, I wanted to take care of you, make you feel special like. Was ready to speak to the judge, But, he didn't need me; you managed just fine on your own, and that got me thinking.

"Am I needed? You've gotten along without me for years. And when it comes to protecting... I'm not sure I'm a proper rescuer. There was no shootout. No kidnapping. Just a lot of legal hoopdedoo."

"And I'm grateful for that," Glinda said firmly. "At my age, getting kidnapped or being in the middle of a gunfight isn't something I want. We had quite enough excitement around my store when those guests of Kent's kept coming in. But in case you'd forgotten, you were there protecting me. Who was it who sat there, rifle at the ready, to defend me and Betty? It was you.

"Truthfully, I'd much rather leave that exciting stuff to the young folks. If I never have another adventurous thing like that happen again, I wouldn't mind. What I want is steady and mature. Like you."

"Eli told me that," he mused. "I guess a feller just likes to feel useful, and I was worried that I weren't that way."

"You are more than useful," Glinda told him, reaching over to take his arm. "You saved my store, Gus. You saved me."

He squinted at her. "Reckon I helped a little."

"Reckon you were the one who found just the evidence to show Mr. Thomas was dishonest, and was able to get that proof into the hands of those who needed it. Who ordered the judge be sent for? Who made it back here, that information safe and saw it to the sheriff?"

"Was followed too," he added nonchalantly, not mentioning it had been by Billy. He'd have to make sure the young gunslinger never said a word. "Set a trap to catch them if they came after me." Gus shrugged. "Lucky for him, I didn't."

Glinda told him, her eyes adoring as she held his hand, "Gus, there's something you need to know. My heart has belonged to you since the moment I met you. I love you for who you are, not just the things you do. You are the one I've waited so long for, and that I'd like to call my own."

"Then, why are we still waiting?" Gus asked. "How 'bout it?"

"How about what?" Glinda asked.

Gus took a deep breath. "We'll figure things out with the ranch and your store, since we both work. But since we two agree we've waited long enough, and well, winter's coming and I might not get to see you for a few weeks if we get snow trapped..."

She raised her eyebrows slightly, and then something Billy had once told him came to mind. How women liked sweet words, and how you needed to be real specific with what you were saying, even if it made you feel a little silly.

Judging by the look on her face—the same one that mule of his used to wear—this was the time to use those sweet words and also explain a little better where his thoughts were heading.

He cleared his throat and tried again, "What I mean is, I don't want to spend a minute away from you that I don't have to. That I love you, Glinda. Always have, always will, and I'm hoping you'll do me the privilege of being my sweetheart and one day my wife."

"I'd like nothing more," Glinda said, smiling up at him. "Perhaps a spring wedding? That gives me winter to make plans and to make a dress." Her cheeks colored, as she admitted, "I never got to do that the first time. We married the night before the wagon train left. There was no pretty dress, no meal with friends, not even a special dessert. Is it silly, I'd love a church wedding with my friends and family there? With a meal afterward?"

"Not silly at all," Gus told her. He added, "You get you the wedding you always dreamed of."

"Is there anything you'd like, especially?" Glinda asked him.

"Don't need nothing but you," Gus told her. "You're all I ever wanted."

Glinda leaned over and kissed him then, and Gus thought his heart was about to fall out of his chest the way it exploded. Maybe living in town near the doc wouldn't be a bad idea. Seems his ticker was doing a lot of jolting as of late.

When they broke apart, he said, "Woowee. Glinda, I love you more than Madge's apple pie."

She laughed at that, and put her head on his shoulder. "I'm glad to hear that. But how about I ask her to make some of her pies for our wedding?"

Gus sniffled, and his eyes burned something fierce. He wasn't rightly sure why.

"Are you all right?" Glinda asked worriedly, looking up at him.

"Reckon I am," Gus said, a little surprised when something warm trickled out of his eye. "Seems I'm so happy right now, I'm crying."

Glinda laughed, and put her head back against his shoulder. "I'm not going to ask if it's the wedding plans or the pie. I don't think I want to know."

"Oh, it's you, no doubt," Gus told her. But then, because he just couldn't lie, admitted, "But I do love me some of Madge's pies."

Epilogue

One month later

They'd finished eating about an hour before. Now, Hannah and her family, along with Billy and Mirabelle, Nora and Aiden, Callie and Ryan, who'd just made it back to Red Ridge the day before, and Gavin's family were talking in small clusters as the sun started to set. Betty had been invited, but was dining with Kent at the hotel.

Gavin's fiddle was playing one of Glinda's favorite songs, and she found herself humming along. Gus was next to her, tapping his toes. "Love this one," he said. "You remember it?"

She glanced at him, furrowing her brow. Before she could answer, though, Gus said, "That traveling band was playing it the first time I ever saw you."

Her breath caught. "So they were," she murmured. "Your mind is so sharp, Gus."

"All them newspapers. I like keeping up with things," Gus said. "When you stop a learning, you start getting old."

"I quite agree," she said, thinking back to the books she enjoyed reading each evening after her work was done.

Though it had only been a month since they'd started courting, she and Gus had fallen into it quite naturally. She supposed that's what a friendship decades long did. Made a body comfortable with another.

"Gus! Can you give me a hand with that harmonica of yours?" Gavin called.

"Sure can," Gus answered and stood. As Gus reached for it in his pocket, she caught a flash of lace. "Is that my handkerchief?" she asked, eyes wide.

"Mine," he corrected her. "You done told me to keep it, and that's just what I did. Carry it with me every day."

Her lips curved into a smile, and she watched as he danced over to Gavin, and the two of them, with Winnie's younger brother Nick joining in with a guitar, played another song.

"I look forward to the wedding," Hannah said, sitting next to her.

"So do I," Glinda said. "I am glad too, that we found the perfect solution. Gus helping me three days a week at the store, and three days on the ranch. He'd miss being here too much."

"I'm glad he's willing to train one of the hands who he thinks would make a good foreman, so that when the day comes, he feels better about his leaving, and Eli and I do too. Not that," Hannah hastily added, "we want anything other than his happiness. I meant that I didn't want Gus worrying."

"I understand," Glinda said. "You're his family. Soon to be mine."

Hannah reached for her hands. "You stood by me, kept my children fed by selling to me when everything was going on. You were my family right then, and I'll always be so grateful for you."

Hot tears pricked Glinda's eyes, and she said, "Just did what anybody should have done."

"Should have," Hannah repeated, "but didn't."

"All's well that ends well," Gus said, coming up and hearing the end of their conversation. "After all, I done sent away for that gunslinger, didn't I? Just a lucky bonus he brought along them other fellers to fatten up the town."

"Yes, you did," Hannah laughed. "And I agree."

"My Gus," Glinda said. "Always saving the day."

Just then, Billy shouted. "The baby's coming!"

Everyone gasped, and started running toward Mirabelle, who stood there, eyes wide and holding her stomach.

"Good thing the doctor's here," Nora said with a laugh. "I'll fetch your bag, Aiden!"

As Mirabelle was taken into the house, Glinda glanced over at Gus who was pushing his lips out.

"What are you thinking about?" she asked.

"How reckon I won't never be no pa, but I'm mighty glad. Rather claim the little 'uns as family. Don't think my heart can take the strain of raising one."

He pointed to Billy, who was as white as the shirt Gavin was wearing. Eli was laughing at Billy, who was now protesting that this was a hundred times worse than that time in Utah.

"You don't realize it," Glinda whispered to him, "but every single one of them thinks of you as their pa or uncle or grandpa. Don't have to be blood born to be family."

"Reckon that's a right nice thing," Gus said. "Care to dance?"

She took his hand, and a short time later, to everyone's surprise, Nora came out from the house waving her arms. "It's a girl!" she called, and then ran back inside.

"When the cheers died down a little, Ryan called out, "Don't worry, Billy! Kept my promise, and got you a double gunbelt."

Everyone still outside the house laughed, and congratulations started.

"Trouble, that's what that little one's going to be," Gus decided.

"And I'm sure glad we're going to be together to see it," Glinda said, wrapping her arm through his.

And it was true. Glinda had the feeling they'd be seeing a lot of things together. After all, the town of Red Ridge was never quiet for too long.

***

What's next?

Red Ridge is filled with Christmas wishes, but the biggest ones of all might come from strangers seeking shelter. But is that too tall of an order? It might be, when the secret they harbor could lead to the town burning.

Read the final story in the Red Ridge Chronicles: *The Christmas Wedding*.

But don't worry...more Red Ridge adventures are on the way. In the meantime, get ready for a new series, set in the small town of Deepwater, Missouri, with the friends you already know, like Maggie, Reverend Sullivan, Laura, Alyssa, and many others.

Start reading The Christmas Wedding now.

***

Claim your bonus story!

When an old friend calls, legendary gunslingers Eli Jones, Billy Madison, and Gavin Jefferson answer without hesitation. They've faced down the toughest outlaws, always bringing justice with deadly precision and no remorse. But nothing could prepare them for the fiery Stella, a woman determined to blaze her own trail—even at risk to one of their own.

Start reading The Riders now.

Note from Author

Thank you for taking the time to read *The Old Man.* Could I ask for one small favor? Reviews like yours on Amazon mean so much to me and help others to find my books! Even just a single line means a lot!

Also...

Want a FREE book?

Stop by my website to get your no strings attached **FREE book**. It's my gift to you, as a thank you for reading this one.

www.sarahlambbooks.com

Want a Free Red Ridge Chronicles Prequel?

Enjoy the gunslingers' adventure that happens just before Eli answers Hannah's ad.

The Riders

When an old friend calls, legendary gunslingers Eli Jones, Billy Madison, and Gavin Jefferson answer without hesitation. They've faced down the toughest outlaws, always bringing justice with deadly precision and no remorse. But nothing could prepare them for the fiery Stella, a woman determined to blaze her own trail—even at risk to one of their own.

As they race to prevent a catastrophe, the trio soon realizes that love is a more dangerous adversary than any outlaw.

These quick-draw, sharp-witted gunslingers have always sworn off settling down, but what happens next might just change their minds.

Discover the electrifying prequel to the Red Ridge Chronicles, a historical romance series in ebook, paperback, large print, and audiobook.

Read it in ebook here:

https://dl.bookfunnel.com/dt01yp1w38

Listen to it in audiobook here:

https://dl.bookfunnel.com/bq8tiktnwu

Read or Listen to the Red Ridge Chronicles Books

Amazon: https://www.amazon.com/dp/B0DQ7HFQ15
Audible:
https://www.audible.com/author/Sarah-Lamb/B098H3
SGLK

Book 1

The Gunslinger

Book 2

The Drifter

Book 3

The Lawman

Book 4

The Doctor

Book 5

The Tracker

Book 6

The Newcomer

Book 7

The Old Man

Book 8

The Christmas Wedding

About the Author

Sarah writes captivating characters and clean romance that's anything BUT boring! From heartbreaking moments to heartwarming tales, get swept away in either historical or small town romance that pulls you in until the last page.

Nestled in the Blue Ridge Mountains of Virginia where she's married to her Texan husband, you'll find Sarah creating her next book, spending time with her children, or volunteering in her community.

Want more of Sarah's books? Find them all on Amazon!

https://www.amazon.com/stores/Sarah-Lamb/author/B098H3SGLK

www.ingramcontent.com/pod-product-compliance
Lightning Source LLC
La Vergne TN
LVHW090947080826
845145LV00003B/918

* 9 7 8 1 9 6 0 4 1 8 6 7 8 *